The Wrong Woman
by
Jane Retzig

The Wrong Woman

First Published 2015

ISBN – 13:978-1506084404
ISBN – 10:1506084400
© Jane Retzig 2015

This novel is a work of fiction. Names, characters, places and incidents are either products of the author's imagination or are used fictitiously. Any other resemblance to actual events, locations or persons, living or dead, is entirely coincidental.

All rights reserved. Except for review, no part of this book may be reproduced in any form without permission in writing from the author.
janeretzig@gmail.com

For MDMK & TBD
With Love

THE WRONG WOMAN

It would have been hard to find anywhere less suited to its name than the Horton Hill Deluxe Country Hotel and Conference Centre.

The place looked like a 1960's Secondary Modern School *('Award winning design')* and was located on an industrial estate on the southern edge of the Leeds Outer Ring Road *('Tranquil surroundings, within easy reach of the cosmopolitan capital of West Yorkshire')*. The weed-choked car park had potholes big enough to swallow a small child. And the whole place was heaving with men in suits and women in tight dresses and high heels, tottering round the sinkholes in the direction of what was obviously a wedding party massing at the dilapidated front entrance.

'Jesus wept!!' Kate cursed under her breath at the two SUVs taking up three parking spaces between them, resisted the urge to get out and move a Lambretta into the hedge, and narrowly missed being rammed by a people-carrier full of bridesmaids swerving, in a flash of fuchsia, for the drop-off area outside the main entrance. This took away the option of pulling in, even for a couple of minutes to unload the papers, books, flip chart, and suitcase piled on the back seat of her tiny black C1.

'You have reached your destination' said the Sat Nav for the third time over the hiss of the air con. But it was no good. The car park was full. Three cars had arrived after her. And they were now blocking her in.

Waving impatiently at them to reverse – how on earth could they not see that there was no room? - Kate backed out of the car park entrance after them and finally found a gap thirty car lengths away from the hotel outside a boarded up storage unit with razor-wire fencing. The prospect of still having wheels on the car in the morning was starting to look more and more remote.

'At the first opportunity, turn round' said the Sat Nav.

'Well, *you* can shut up for a start!!!!' Kate jabbed the off switch and buried her head in her hands. How the hell was she going to manage a conference on 'Traumatology for the 21st Century' alongside a wedding party that looked like it had just stepped out of some Yorkshire version of 'The Only Way is Essex'?

She was hot. She was sweaty. She had the mother of all headaches. She was only *holding* the blasted conference here because the Northern members had moaned so much about the organisation being 'London-centric'. And now here she was, on her own, in the back of beyond with a carload of stuff to carry down the street and into that awful hovel of a hotel.

Still, she hadn't got to be the youngest ever (heading up to thirty next birthday) organiser of the Annual Conference of the UK Institute of Trauma Therapists by giving up at the first hurdle. And, she told herself, it really was not necessary to fall prey to any of those random negative thoughts that were flashing into her mind right now.

'Just stop right there!' she said firmly to the thought that everything was going to be awful.

'But it *is!'* said the thought with conviction.

'It doesn't *have* to be,' said Kate, losing ground slightly.

'It does – it's going to be a ***disaster***' said the thought.

Kate knew that if completely over-the-top words like 'disaster' were starting to make an appearance, her anxiety levels were far too high for thought-stopping.

She wondered if distraction might work better.

She climbed out of the car and found her reflection looking wearily back at her from the side window. She'd seen a client first thing that morning and had finally managed to get away from London just before eleven o'clock. But there had been road works and an accident and the journey had taken an hour longer than planned. At Leicester Forest East Services, where she'd stopped for a sandwich and coffee to try to override the afternoon drowsiness that was threatening to engulf her, she had splashed cold water on her face and tied back her hair. It looked limp now, reflecting, pretty accurately, how she was feeling. Her clothes appeared to have given up on her too. She tried to smooth the wrinkles out of the linen trousers she'd worn because she thought they'd be cool to travel in. Thankfully, she had a travel iron in her case. Kate liked to travel well prepared for eventualities such as these.

She'd opened the back door of the car and pulled her case half off the seat, wondering if she could manage the flip chart in her other hand when the syncopated thud of 'Salute' by Little Mix throbbed towards her on the hot, mid afternoon air. The music was accompanied by the low rattle of a van engine that sounded like it was on its last legs. Kate knew without looking that it was going to be white. Her sense of superiority at the idea of X Factor manufactured pop music and 'white van man' made her feel better than she'd felt since she arrived. Then the engine and Little Mix stopped, suddenly, just in front of her. And she looked up, startled, to see who it was that she'd been looking down on.

She was surprised to find that her 'white van man' was, in fact, a woman. A surprisingly attractive woman at that - though Kate pushed that thought from her mind so quickly she hardly even noticed that it had been there. Instead, as the new arrival jumped out of the van and walked towards her, she noticed the grubby white T-shirt, baggy blue jeans and scuffed hi-top trainers that, teamed with a snapback baseball cap with the word SWAG emblazoned on the front (what on earth did that *mean* anyway?) and small butterfly tattooed on her wrist, added up to a vaguely hip-hoppy kind of look. If Rihanna had a secret half-sister who lived in some slum in West Yorkshire, Kate thought, she might just possibly look a little bit like the young woman, maybe in her early-twenties, standing in front of her now.

She might *sound* a bit like her too...

'A' y'stain at 'otel?' she asked in a broad Leeds accent, as she lunged towards Kate's case with the look of someone about to snatch it up and run away with it.

Kate's hand tightened for a moment on the handle, then, despising herself instantly, she forced herself to relax.

She was trying to fathom out what this overly friendly newcomer had just said to her.

'I'm sorry?' she said. 'I didn't quite get that.'

White van woman nodded sympathetically. 'Are you staying at the hotel?' she asked, slowly, and rather loudly, like people do when they're talking to foreigners.

Her voice still held the flat vowels of a broad Yorkshire accent. But at least now she was using words that could be found in The Oxford English Dictionary.

Kate nodded. 'Yes,' she said. 'I couldn't find a space in the car park, so I've ended up here.'

The young woman gave another sympathetic nod. 'I know. It's mad over there, ever since Rodley Grange went down with that vomiting bug. I've just been to the Cash and Carry to make sure we've got enough food in for you all. I'll take your stuff over for you. I can drop it at the back entrance.'

She reached down and picked up the case, heaving open the van door and putting it gently inside. 'If you just hand it to me, I'll pop it all in here,' she said. 'I'm Naz, by the way. I work at Horton Hill. I'm out of uniform at the moment... don't like going out in it, but I'm their "Hospitality Assistant".... otherwise known as General Dogsbody.' She paused, as if expecting Kate to introduce herself too.

Kate let the silence hang as long as she could. She really would have preferred not to have to make conversation. Particularly with someone who should come with English language subtitles. But she couldn't find it in herself to blank Naz's open friendliness.

'Kate Ferrings,' she said reluctantly. 'I'm here for the UKITT conference. I'm the organiser.'

Something indecipherable flickered over Naz's face.

'Well, everybody's welcome at Horton Hill,' she said, after the briefest of pauses. 'Hop in and I'll take you round with your stuff.'

The receptionist was short, bleached-blonde and sturdy. Her white blouse bore a name tag with her photograph and 'Saskia Prochazka' – Horton Hill' typed on it. She gave Kate and Naz a stunning smile as she looked up from the elderly computer she had been studying, seemingly undisturbed by the wall of sound emanating from the crush of wedding guests in the lobby.

'Good aftnoon Mam,' she said in an accent with a strong underlay of something Eastern European. 'Welcome to Horton Hill. Have you reservation book?'

Kate hesitated. She was beyond exhaustion. She tended to hear things literally. And the idea of a reservation book had thrown her.

Naz stepped in to translate. 'It's okay Saskia,' she said. 'She's with the UKIP conference.'

'UKITT!' said Kate, mortified. 'Two T's – for tango.'

'Tango?' Saskia raised an eyebrow in Naz's direction for clarification.

'The United Kingdom Institute of Trauma Therapists,' said Kate, desperate to redeem herself.

'Ah – conference with dance!' She studied the screen. 'No dance book.'

'No! No dance. Just conference...' Kate stopped, embarrassed, realising that she'd just inadvertently copied the receptionist's accent.

Naz leaned over the counter. 'There,' she said, pointing to Saskia's computer screen. 'Kathryn Ferrings – Room 59, plus conference room and audio visual hire... No dance! I'll take your stuff up while Saskia gets you booked in.'

By the time she returned, the members of the wedding party were being ushered into a large room to the left of the hotel lobby, and Kate was gathering together her credit card, electronic room key and shoulder bag. The bridesmaids had re-appeared, chattering like a flock of overexcited starlings around the bride. Naz noticed that one of them was giving her more than a cursory once-over. She blushed.

'All done!' said Saskia brightly.

Kate wondered if she could justify resting her throbbing head for a couple of hours before anyone else arrived.

'Everything's in your room,' said Naz, hoping to regain her attention. Kate was very much her ideal woman, all neat and buttoned up and a bit prim looking. She reminded her of the secretaries and librarians in the old black and white movies she used to watch with her Nan when she was little – waiting for the moment, close to the end of the film, when they would take off their glasses and shake down their hair and reveal the beauty the hero had been much too stupid to notice before.

'Thank you.' Kate barely even glanced at her. She headed wearily for the stairs, ignoring Saskia's suggestion that she could take the lift.

The fire door banged after her as she went through it.

Saskia shrugged and looked at Naz. 'Foreign?' she asked.

'No – just a Southerner.'

'Ah!' The receptionist nodded gravely and went back to her computer screen. 'Fuckable though,' she added, as if out of nowhere. 'I call you if she ask for room service.'

She didn't. Late that night, as she lay in her tiny room in the staff block behind the hotel, Naz wondered about the pull she'd felt towards Kate Ferrings.

It wasn't as if the woman had given her any encouragement. She'd been distant, (bordering on rude), grumpy and a bit patronising. But quite apart from the obvious physical attraction, there was something about her that made Naz want to take care of her - a vulnerability that the smart clothes and superior attitude seemed designed to hide. She'd seen it in the closed down, tired and lost look of the woman as she ate a sandwich alone in the hotel bar, bombarded by the music from the wedding reception, glancing nervously towards the door until, suddenly her face lit up and she pushed back her chair to greet a very tall, once dark, and still handsome older man, who put his hand comfortingly on her arm and whispered something in her ear that seemed to make her feel better.

Naz didn't make a habit of watching the guests too obviously. You had to be alert for if they needed anything of course. But she'd realised very early on that too much attention made them feel nervous and claustrophobic. Over the years she'd developed a kind of sixth sense about when to notice something and when to just phase it out. It was like the way people could just drive on auto pilot until they needed to make an emergency stop.

But she couldn't help watching Kate. She could see that she wasn't happy until the man came. Then it was as if everything was alright. She wondered initially if they were partners, though there was a big age gap between them and Kate was booked into a single room. Maybe lovers then? Having an affair they didn't want other people to know about? Or maybe, just good friends as they laughed together setting out the chairs and side tables in the room they'd be using for the conference tomorrow.

Dotting about the hotel in her evening-shift uniform of white shirt and black trousers... collecting glasses, fixing a broken light in the Ladies', administering First Aid to one of the wedding guests who'd got very drunk, very quickly, and fallen over.... Naz watched out of the corner of her eye as Kate greeted the people who had begun to arrive for her conference. There was an elderly, bearded, and rather eccentric looking man in socks and sandals. Then a wiry American guy in smart grey pants and sports jacket, and a striking looking woman with a South African accent, a big, wavy sweep of dark chestnut hair and a silk jacket in shades of turquoise, pink and navy... About thirty of the UKITT group were booked in for that night. The rest were due to arrive in the morning, travelling direct from home, staying elsewhere if they had any sense.... or just staying over on the Saturday night.

Most of tonight's arrivals seemed to know the handsome man too.

'Do you think he's her boyfriend?' Naz asked Saskia as she took a rare couple of minutes off mid evening, to lean on the reception desk for a moment and get a second opinion from her friend.

'No!... Queer as fuck!'

'Which? Him? Or her?'

'Both!'

Naz wasn't so sure. She didn't have Saskia's downright way of seeing the world. She had to admit that there was a part of her that *wanted* Kate to be gay though.... even if the woman was never likely to look twice at somebody like *her*.

She lay now, remembering how apologetic Kate had been with her guests, embarrassed by the venue. Naz had grown used to the shabbiness of it all. The slight smell of damp in the conference room; the mould on the ceiling; the menu of pizza and chips and scampi in the bar and curled up sliced-white ham or cheese sandwiches with a few crisps on the side for the buffet lunches. The hotel trundled along okay with its regular guests - contractors, lower-end business travellers, ISA groups, and Speed Awareness courses. But seeing Kate so obviously mortified by the place had made her see just how shabby it all must look to an outsider.

Naz hadn't wanted to end her shift that night, desperate to do what tiny things she could to keep the place clean and running as smoothly as she could manage. Almost all of the staff team had been working, and they were generally a good crowd, so they'd had a laugh too. But it was physically hard work with everything packed just slightly beyond capacity. Her twelve hour shift had stretched into fourteen and now she was tired but far too wired to sleep.

It was hot too and her window was open as far as it would go on its safety catch. She could hear the throb of the wedding reception disco, the usual sounds of guests congregating outside for fresh air and cigarettes, their background chatter punctuated by brief, sharp wafts of laughter.

Then she heard rustling and muffled voices just outside her window, and she realised, with a sinking heart, that Dick Whitlass and his trusty henchman Charlie Cash were out there, doing some Friday night business with Max Pollack from the corner shop.

She had a pretty good idea of what they were getting up to because she had actually seen them one night as she was coming back to her room, surprised enough to stop in her tracks at the sight of the hotel manager and his kitchen porter loading bottles of wine into Pollack's car boot. She'd looked away the minute Charlie glanced up and nudged Whitlass to let him know she was there. She knew better than to challenge them. There had been far too many people like that when she'd been growing up in the children's home, and she'd seen what happened to the kids who 'snitched'. The lad with his ribs kicked in. The girl dragged into the toilet block by a group of the older boys. She saw how nobody intervened to help. She hated it, but she never did anything either. She lived with the memory of that on her conscience.

With Whitlass and Charlie, she knew that by looking away she had signalled that she wouldn't make any trouble for them. She loved her job and she loved her little room. She felt lucky to have them when so many of her friends were on the dole, sharing houses or in nasty bedsits with drug dealers next door. Turning a blind eye to the knowledge that the hotel manager was a petty crook was a small price to pay for a wage, security, and a roof over her head.

It still made her nervous though, hearing the mumble of their voices, closing whatever shady deal they were doing out there. She wished she'd kept her window closed. It would have been worth being hot not to run the risk of them thinking she might have overheard.

She felt lighter when she heard the clunk of Pollack's car boot closing.

But then there were footsteps crunching on the gravel, followed shortly by a knock at her door, and the lightness fled.

Terrified, she slammed her bedside lamp off and shoved her headphones over her ears with shaking hands.

Then she played Capital Radio as loud as she could so she'd be sure not to hear whoever was out there if they knocked again.

Saturday was Saskia's morning off. Lucinda Waterstone looked up sourly from the reception desk as Naz walked into the lobby. She was in a bad mood. She'd only been on duty for an hour and already she'd had an altercation with that 'Little Madam' from the UKITT conference. It was hardly Lucinda's fault that the hotel pool was closed due to an algae problem.... And, for the life of her, she could not understand what had been so stupid about offering a nice aromatherapy massage with Mrs Wilkinson from Morley instead.

It wasn't unusual for Lucinda to be grumpy. She was, as Saskia would say, 'All over fucking place!' She could be nice as pie one minute and in a totally foul mood the next. Naz wondered if it was down to the menopause, a phenomenon one of her house 'aunties' had suffered from quite badly at the home. Saskia was convinced it was because she was in love with the boss. Either way she was having a majorly 'off' day today, and it was pretty clear that *somebody* was going to get it in the neck.

'I've been trying to ring you,' she said, glaring at Naz over the top of the glasses she had to wear these days to read the computer screen. 'Tracey needs you in the breakfast room. She's rushed off her feet.'

She didn't *look* rushed. The room was empty, except for one travelling salesman in a grey Primani suit, reading a copy of the Daily Express over his coffee. At the end of the room, a wall-mounted TV set silently looped through the BBC news with sub-titles. A recording of Lennon and McCartney songs played on a zither issued quietly from speakers just above the kitchen door.

Tracey was topping up a pile of variety pack cereals on the breakfast bar as if she were auditioning for 'The Cube'

'Been dying to know,' she whispered, tucking a stray wisp of her long, maroon-dyed hair behind her ear. 'How did it go with Chelsea last night?'

Naz wondered why she wasn't asking Gareth or one of the other lads who were crazy about football. 'Dunno,' she said. 'I didn't even know they were playing.'

'Hah, hah!' said Tracey. 'Very funny!' she nudged Naz playfully in the ribs. 'But you needn't play the innocent with me. It was me that gave her your room number.... Didn't she come across? She told me she had a "bottle of Malibu" she wanted to share with you.'

Naz remembered the knocking at her door.

'What time was this?' she asked.

'About two o'clock. Don't tell me you were asleep!'

'No... Not for most of the night actually.'

'That's sounding more like it. You had me going there for a minute!' Tracey grinned.

'No... I mean, I heard her knocking and thought it was Mr Whitlass. Nearly scared the shit out of me!'

Concern shot into Tracey's soft green eyes. 'How come you thought it was Whitlass? He's not been pestering you has he? He tried it on with me once at the staff Christmas party. Told him I'd serve him his bollocks for breakfast in a bap if he ever touched me again. Never had a peep out of him since!' Tracey was older than Naz by a couple of years and she'd taken her under her wing from day one. Right now she looked ready to form a lynch mob and hunt down the boss.

'No... God no. Nothing like that! I'd just heard him outside earlier that's all.'

'What? Like lurking around outside your window, you mean?'

'No,' said Naz hastily. 'Just talking to Charlie from the kitchen.'

Tracey looked unconvinced. 'Are you sure about that? I'll have a word with him for you if he's been out of line. It's not on. Not in this day and age. Bloody perve. He's old enough to be your granddad!'

'Thanks T, but honest! He's never touched me. Cross my heart!'

'Or peeped in your window? Or owt like that?'

'No – Honest!'

'Mm! Well he'd better not do either!' Tracey looked indignant. 'So you didn't let Chelsea in then?'

'No. I didn't know it was her. But I couldn't have done anyway. It's against the rules to fraternise with the guests.'

Tracey spluttered. 'Blimey Naz, for a lesbian you are so straight! They don't pay us enough here to expect us to stick to the rules. Haven't you figured that one out yet? How do you think I can afford Jimmy Choo shoes on *my* wage? I don't get the tips I get for serving up the muck they call food in *this* place, *I* can tell you!' As if on cue, Primani man looked up and smiled at her over his newspaper. She rippled her fingers at him in a flirtatious wave.

Naz wasn't sure she'd recognise a Jimmy Choo shoe if it stood on her. So it was news to her to find that Whitlass and Charlie weren't the only ones with an extra income stream at Horton Hill. It made her uncomfortable. She liked rules. They helped her know where she was. But she didn't want to get into a disagreement with Tracey about it. 'So which one was Chelsea?' she asked. She remembered the girl who'd been giving her the glad eye.

'Was she one of the bridesmaids? Short red hair? Blue eyes? Quite cute?'

Tracey nodded. 'You see,' she said. 'You *were* paying attention after all.'

Not really, thought Naz. But she found herself blushing anyway.

At that moment, Kate decided to descend on the breakfast room with four of her entourage.

Naz's heartbeat jolted up a notch, along with her temperature.

'Now, I wouldn't mind breaking the rules for *her*' she said.

Tracey turned to look in amazement. 'You've *got* to be joking!' she said. 'Confzilla? She's a total cow!'

'I don't think she is. I just think she's stressed.'

'Yeah, right. And just because *she's* stressed, she's making everyone else's life a misery. I just heard her having a *right* go at Lucinda out on reception, and let's face it, we can't be doing with Lucinda being in any worse a mood than usual. Trust me love. Steer well clear. I've met her type a hundred times over. 'Specially when I used to work at Rodley Grange. Total diva. "Fetch me... carry me". Thinks she's better than anybody else. She'd lead you a right merry dance. You stick to a nice normal lass like Chelsea. Bet you could still get her phone number when she comes down for breakfast if you play your cards right.'

David Cohen felt concerned as he watched Kate wilting over the breakfast table. Guiltily, he wondered if he had allowed his protégée to push herself too far, too quickly. There was no doubting her ability. He'd seen it immediately when she enrolled on his psychotherapy training straight out of university eight years ago. Head and shoulders above the rest of his students, she was a brilliantly intuitive therapist with a sharp, analytical mind. She'd already been published in several leading journals, and with her first book 'The Hope of Trauma Recovery' well on its way to completion, she was clearly destined for greatness.

The problem was that she didn't project a particularly good image. She charged top dollar for her private work (and David had heard a lot of snide remarks about *that* over the years), and she carried an air of superiority that got people's backs up. It was a shame because she had a good heart. As her supervisor, David knew that she still worked 'pro bono' with clients referred to her from the local women's refuge. Voluntary work was something most therapists did while they were in training, but they usually dropped it when they became accredited and there weren't many of Kate's standing who would still be prepared to do that kind of heartbreaking, horrifying work for nothing.

But proving herself mattered, just a little bit too much for Kate. The status of being Conference Organiser, for instance, was important to her, though in practice, it was a job that no-one else had wanted, being unpaid and largely unappreciated. He knew he'd turned a blind eye to the stresses on her as she took on more and more responsibility within the rapidly growing organisation, just relieved that her eagerness had taken the pressure off him while he nursed his partner Daniel through his final illness and adapted to the grief of heading toward his sixties alone.

This morning though, he couldn't help but notice that she was struggling as she tried to make conversation with

Rosa Frankl, the rather earnest South African neurobiologist who was to be this year's Keynote Speaker. And seeing the dark rings under her eyes, he wondered if he'd possibly been selfish and a bit lazy in not protecting her more.

Certainly, small talk didn't come easily to Kate, and David could see that the change of venue was getting to her more than it needed to. Having organised most of the Institute's conferences, he knew full-well that, provided the speakers were entertaining, the coffee strong, the biscuits okay, and the tea not too stewed, people would be far too busy networking and catching up with old colleagues and acquaintances to notice the grottiness of their surroundings for more than a few passing moments.

'Shall we see what delights are in store for us at the Deluxe Breakfast Buffet?' he asked, lightly, aiming to rescue Kate from her conversation with Rosa. Then, seeing the anguished look that flitted over her face, he kicked himself for his faint ironic dig at the hotel.

They both stood up to allow their guests to go first.

'You look tired,' David said gently, drawing her to one side.

Kate shook her head. 'I'm fine. I struggled to sleep that's all. It was hot and the mattress was lumpy and the wedding reception disco was so noisy. Then I was just drifting off when I was nearly frightened out of my wits by these *terrifying* orgasmic screams from the woman in the next room. Dear God, I thought she was being *murdered*!' Kate wondered if she should also tell David about the text she'd received from a client at 4.30am. These texts were starting to become a habit and she knew that, as her supervisor, David should be kept in the loop about them. But she'd made him laugh, so she decided against it.

'Speaking of orgasmic screams,' he chuckled. 'Do you know you've got an admirer?'

Kate followed his gaze to where Naz was standing by the cereal stack, very obviously discussing her with her colleague. The younger woman looked away quickly as their eyes met.

'I don't think so,' said Kate. She felt her face growing hot. Then she felt unreasonably irritated with Naz for being the source of her embarrassment. 'We got off to a bad start. She thought I was from UKIP.'

This made David laugh even more. 'Well,' he grinned. 'She's pretty gorgeous, and she's obviously forgiven you for looking like a member of the lunatic right. If I were twenty years younger she might even tempt *me* to give up the habits of a lifetime while I'm stuck in this godforsaken place.'

Kate knew what he was doing. He was hinting that she needed to 'lighten up' – have a little fun. But she'd given up on the idea of having fun a long time ago. In fact, if she was entirely honest, people having 'fun' seemed a bit silly and irritating to her.

'She's hardly likely to be *my* type, now, is she?' she said defensively, implying that, if she *had* 'a type' it would be someone with a whole lot more going on intellectually than the girl who'd just blushed when she caught her eye across the room. 'And anyway, you *know* I'm married to my work.'

'Well, you shouldn't be,' David sighed. 'It isn't good for you.... And it isn't good for the work either.' Sadly, he could imagine Kate's 'type'; Dull academics, unlikely to ever consider getting steamy under the sheets. He knew she identified as lesbian because she'd written a paper about it. But if she'd ever had a significant other, he'd never seen them.

Secretly, he wondered if the bright, attractive and sweet (if only she'd allow herself to be) young woman at his side had ever had a proper romantic relationship in her life.

The first day of the conference was a huge success. Rosa came alive in front of her audience, bamboozling them with science and stunning colour brain scans that wouldn't have looked out of place in the Tate Modern. Dominic Fuller (sports jacket/smart trousers) was witty and engaging as he updated them all on the latest trials with bilateral stimulation. And Jim Crowe (aged hippy - socks and sandals) brought the obligatory elder statesman authority to the 3.30pm 'graveyard' session when most of the audience were nodding off.

All that remained for Sunday morning was the formal AGM of the Institute, so by 5pm the conference room was buzzing with the excited chatter of people discussing what they were going to do with their evening off.

Kate always felt shy during these social parts of the proceedings and in her early days at conferences, would have quietly slipped away to order a club sandwich from room service, fix herself a small gin and tonic from the mini bar and watch TV until it was a reasonable time to go to bed.

Tonight, she knew she'd be dining with David and the other speakers, hopefully somewhere in Leeds where there might be a hope of a decent restaurant. But that was unlikely to be before 7pm, so she felt at a bit of a loss, temporarily, hovering by the side tables, loading books and papers into boxes while David's easy laughter crowd-surfed towards her over the babble of voices in the room.

'Are you taking those out to the car?'

Kate looked up, surprised, to find Naz at her elbow, looking at her with her big, striking, brown eyes.

She was surprised to realise that she was pleased to see her.

'No, I thought I'd take them back up to my room for now.... I was going to move my car into the car park, but the Star Trek convention had arrived before I got round to it.'

Shuddering a little, she recalled her shock at coming face to face with her first two 'Klingons' of the morning, coming into the lobby as she was about to go out.

Naz noticed, and smiled. 'We should have warned you,' she said. 'They can be a bit unnerving if you're not expecting them..... Anyway, I'll help you up with these then, shall I?'

'No – no truly – I'm fine!'

Naz ignored her and picked up the box. Clearly the 'shall I?' had just been some strange Yorkshire figure of speech.

Kate snatched up the second of the boxes and half-ran after her helper, noticing with a sinking heart that she was making a bee-line for the service lift.

'I'll just head up the stairs with these,' called Kate. 'I'm sure the hotel insurance won't cover guests getting in there.'

'Don't be daft,' said Naz, genially, taking the box from her. 'We take people in wheelchairs up in it all the time.... people with serious obesity problems too. It's bigger than the other one.'

'Right....' Kate hesitated, feeling the familiar dread washing through her. She forced herself to breathe but something very heavy was pushing against her chest.

Naz was waiting for her.

Kate wondered which would be worse. Stepping into the lift or admitting to just how terrified she was of stepping into it.

Seeing her hesitation, Naz remembered how Kate had always taken the stairs, even when she'd looked half dead on her feet.

'Hey, you're not phobic or anything are you?' she asked.

'No... not at all. Of course not!'

'Well there's no shame in it. I'm really scared of moths and I know it's daft.'

Yes, well you're not a trauma therapist! Kate wanted to scream. But she didn't. This was something she'd never admitted to anyone... always tried to deal with herself.

She walked into the lift.

Instantly, she felt like the floor was coming up to meet her. Her lungs refused to take in air. She told herself it would only be a couple of minutes.

'Okay,' said Naz, pulling the metal doors across.

Kate clamped her hands over her mouth to bury the scream that began to form the moment the outside world disappeared from view.

The lift began to judder upwards.

It was too much.

Beyond rational thought, she lurched towards the control panel and jabbed at the emergency button, over and over, deaf to Naz's voice shouting something, heedless of the hands that were trying, first gently, then increasingly forcefully, to stop her.

The light went out and the lift slammed to a halt, felt like it was swaying for a moment, then was still.

'Well,' said Naz, in the darkness somewhere on the periphery of Kate's consciousness. '*That* was daft!'

'Well, thank you *very* much!!!' Fury surged in Kate's chest... followed immediately by a horrible sense of nausea.

Feeling for the cold metal wall of the lift behind her, she allowed herself to sink slowly down into a sitting position on the floor and wondered if she really, actually was going to be sick.

Naz hunted in her pocket for her mobile and switched the torch facility on. She checked, holding the phone in all directions, high and low, to see if she could get a signal, though she knew it would be useless. The last person to get stuck wouldn't have been in there for four hours if they'd been able to phone out. Miserably, she hunkered down beside Kate in the dim torchlight. 'Hey,' she said, softly. 'I'm sorry. We'll be okay. It's just a fuse that's blown. We'll be out of here in no time when they realise that we're missing.'

Kate looked wildly at her through her tears. 'You mean there's no alarm in here?' she asked.

Naz thought it was best to tell the truth. 'There *should* be,' she confessed. 'But it doesn't work.'

'*And you use it for carrying people in wheelchairs and the clinically obese? Have you people never heard of Health and Safety?!*'

'Well people don't generally go jabbing at the emergency button like somebody demented.'

Kate shook her head, holding onto her skull through her hair, as if she were frightened that something might explode if she didn't keep a very firm grip on it. 'This whole fucking place is a death trap!' she muttered to herself. She could smell fear on herself and she was sure Naz must smell it too. It just added to the utter humiliation of it all.

Naz stood up. 'Let's see if anyone can hear us,' she said. Her head was clearing now from the shock of Kate's meltdown and she could see that somebody needed to take control of the situation.

She pointed herself towards the doors and yelled at the top of her voice. *'HELLO!... HI!... ANYBODY?... CAN ANYBODY HEAR ME?...'*

Very faintly, from the lobby came what sounded like an answering cheer.

Kate's heart lurched with hope. 'Was that?....' she asked desperately. 'Can they?....'

The cheering grew louder, accompanied by the theme tune from 'Star Trek Voyager.'

Naz looked at her watch. 'Nope,' she said. 'Unfortunately, I reckon that'll be the mystery guest arriving for the Trekkies.'

She pictured the surge towards the entrance doors as one of the stars (usually fairly minor) of the TV show drew up in a limousine outside. The excitement, and noise levels down there would be hitting fever pitch as people jostled to make out the face behind the privacy glass and see which of their heroes would be joining them for the evening.

One by one, she accounted for the hotel staff in her head... Whitlass would be in the lobby in his suit, smiling benevolently around the throng as if he'd organised it all himself. Saskia had taken over from Lucinda about an hour ago, but she'd be pretty much glued to her reception desk staring at 'Fucking morons!' as if this were just an

English phenomenon. The kitchen staff along with Tracey and all her team would be busy with the buffet; Picard Pie this year, along with the traditional giant Enterprise cake on the top table. And the chambermaids would have long since hung up their dusters and gone home to their families.

'Guess your mates at the conference are going to miss you pretty quickly?' she asked hopefully.

Kate shook her head. She doubted it. And she was clearly hyperventilating.

'Hey, come on now... just try to relax.' Naz knelt again and reached a tentative hand out to touch Kate's arm.

She swatted it away. 'Don't you think I would if I could?' she demanded.

Naz gritted her teeth. For a moment, she wondered if Tracey may have been right about this woman. Then she remembered the terror she had seen in Kate's reaction to the closing doors, and searching desperately for inspiration, she remembered her Nan. Not the horrible final images that still sometimes kept her awake at night. The cancer and the awful effects of the treatment. But the earlier, happier times... the scent of rose and patchouli, warm blue eyes, wild hair, tie dye T-shirts, cheap, hippy bangles and beads....

'I was a really nervous kid,' she said, about to go on when Kate interrupted her.

'That surprises me. You seem so confident now.'

'I'm not confident.'

'Well, you seem it.... Confident and... and upbeat.'

'Well... anyway.... When I was a kid and I'd get frightened about things, my Nan used to get me singing, like in The Sound of Music.'

Please don't make me sing 'My Favourite Things'... I'm already feeling stupid enough.

'You know... like when Julie Andrews is walking along with her guitar case singing 'I Have Confidence.''

Not that one either... please!

'I can't sing,' said Kate hastily. 'I sound like a bag of cats!'

'I bet you don't.'

'Trust me!' Kate closed her eyes. She noticed that her heart rate had slowed a little and her lungs seemed to be coming out of their temporary state of partial-paralysis. She wanted Naz to keep talking. It helped. But she certainly, definitely, absolutely did ***not*** want to sing.

'How come you were a nervous kid?' she asked, falling automatically into role. She was good at keeping the spotlight on other people. It always worked for her in her job. It even sometimes worked in social situations, though it wasn't very conducive to making equal relationships. It seemed worth a try now.

'It's a long story.'

'We might be here a long time.' Oh God, why had she just said that? Her heart accompanied the statement with a drum roll.

'Hopefully not! I'll try shouting again when it quietens down out there.'

Thank you!

Kate waited, wondering if Naz would fill the silence like people usually did.

'My mum had a drug and alcohol problem,' she said. 'My Nan got custody of me.'

'That sounds tough!'

'Not really. Nan was great.... Hey... Are you trying to psychoanalyse me?'

The drum roll switched to a more syncopated beat as Kate realised she'd been rumbled.

'No... Look, I'm sorry. It's a habit.'

'Yeah... well it's not me that's having a panic attack here now, is it?' Instantly Naz could have bitten her tongue. But it was too late. Beside her, she felt Kate flinch. 'I'm sorry,' she said.

'No,' Kate shook her head. 'You're right. This is my fault. And it's me that's behaving like a nervous wreck. I'm just not great with enclosed spaces - that's all. I should never have let you persuade me to get into the lift.'

'What's the deal with enclosed spaces?'

'Are *you* trying to psychoanalyse *me* now?'

'Maybe.'

For a second, Kate hesitated. She'd never talked about this. She'd never wanted to. Bizarrely, she'd even managed to avoid it in the five years of therapy that had been a compulsory part of her training. She'd avoided it because she hadn't wanted to talk about what came after. She figured that was why she'd never managed to shake herself free of it.

In her mind she could see the cellar room as clearly as it was then, the tea-light flickering and casting terrifying shadows over the work bench, the hooks on the walls where the tools had hung, the dark stain on the stone floor where they'd told her he died.

She began to sweat.

In the real world, Kate felt Naz's hand slide on top of hers, gently, and she remembered the cobwebs. The sound of scuttling in the corners. The cold of the salt-pocked walls damp against her duffle coat.... seeping, it seemed, into the very marrow of her bones.

She felt tears running slowly down her cheeks, just as they had then, except then the tears had chilled on her face, leaving it sore, and stopping her crying out of self preservation.

She remembered the smell of mildew, and damp wood and mice.

The toilet corner hidden under a piece of old sacking.

Nowhere to wash her hands.

Ironically, she'd sung hymns to herself back then for courage. But that was in the old days, when she still believed in God.

Naz's hand was warm on hers. Comforting.

'It's okay,' she said. 'You don't have to talk about it if you don't want to.'

There are some places that are just beyond words. Naz knew that. Her hand tightened protectively over Kate's, who remembered the spiteful laughter....

'Ferret... Hey Ferret! Where's your granddad, where's your grandma? Oh no, I'm sorry that's your dad, isn't it? That's your mum? Why don't you recite The Bible for us? Let's just copy your homework... Give us your dinner money Ferret, or we'll put you in the cellar.'

Kate remembered her stupid, teenage infatuation with the ringleader, Rachel Stiles, who was beautiful and blonde, with breasts and an older boyfriend called Mike who drove a black Volkswagen Golf. You think you can hide your feelings about these things, but you can't. There's the stammering and the blushes. The secret fantasies that someday somebody like Rachel will see you for who you really are and make you their best friend. They show in your eyes, those fantasies. People see them in you and they use them against you.

They use *any* weakness against you.

And she could hear it in her imagination, the laughter.... Rachel's never loud like the rest, but quieter, in the background. And there was something triumphant in it.... something chilling.

The feeling of dread, like a lift going down, leaving your stomach behind....

She knew she couldn't talk about it. It was too hard to talk about, even to a stranger. Kate wished she could do the EFT technique that helped sometimes when it all came back to her, but it was hard to start tapping at yourself without looking like a complete weirdo. She focused back on trying to steady her breathing.

And in the end, she gave in. 'Okay then,' she said, with something of a return to her normal voice. 'Are you going to teach me your Nan's song, or what?'

In the conference room, people had begun to drift toward showers, calls home, and preparations for going out.

David headed over to Jim Crowe, who was disentangling himself from a small group of admirers. The old man had Jammy Dodger crumbs from the afternoon tea-break in his beard.

'Nice talk,' David said, though if he was being honest, he'd been disappointed with it. Recently, he thought, Jim's presentations had become a bit lazy and predictable. Pretty much like his last two books, come to think of it, which were really no more than rehashed transcripts of lectures that had seemed incredibly new and exciting once.

Jim gave a slow, self-satisfied nod. 'Always give the public what they want, that's what *I* always say.

So, he knew what he was doing then. David wasn't sure whether that made it better, or worse. But he knew that being with Jim made him feel old and jaded.

'Are you going to join us for dinner?' he asked. 'I thought we could go into Leeds. There's a nice vegetarian Indian Restaurant there apparently. It's got good write ups.'

'Who's we? Is Kate coming?'

'Yes, Kate and Rosa and Dominic...'

They were following the general flow of people out of the room and towards the lift, which had a massive queue of Trekkies around it.

David raised an eyebrow. 'Shall we use the stairs?'

'I think so. People in uniform make me nervous.... So, what's the story with Kate?'

'What do you mean?' he paused briefly to face Jim full-on. He knew what his old friend and mentor was like. And he'd seen that look before.

The older man was unfazed. 'Is she in a relationship? I never see her with anyone.'

'You're old enough to be her granddad, Jim.' He could feel himself bridling, though he wasn't entirely sure why. Kate, after all, was old enough to look after herself. And perfectly capable of telling this dirty old man where to get off.

'I could be very good for her career.'

'You could be good for her career *without* shagging her, you old goat!' He was surprised at how furious he felt.

'Oh, come on DC – you can't tell me you never exercised droit du seigneur with some of those pretty boys you taught back in the eighties.'

'No, I bloody didn't Jim. I wouldn't. And I was with Daniel by then, as well you know!'

Jim looked languidly amused. His pale blue eyes twinkled. Winding David up had always been one of his favourite sports. 'Well we all know what you gay guys are like. You probably *both* had 'em, if truth be known.'

'You're really pissing me off now Jim!'

'Well, that's what friends are for isn't it?... To spook your high horse. Just think how insufferably pompous you'd be if I wasn't around to remind you of your baser human nature from time to time. But, seriously, I'm interested in all this protective Big Daddy stuff about Kate. Massive dose of countertransference going on there, if I'm not mistaken.'

David wasn't listening.... Or not to Jim anyway...

He'd stopped in his tracks.

'Shut up a minute!' he said.

'I beg your...'

'Shush!' David raised his finger to his lips and cocked his head. They were standing by the service lift. And he could hear singing.

'What does that sound like to you?' he asked.

Jim listened. 'Sounds like "Born to Be Wild"' he said, starting to nod his head along with the song. In his mind, he was instantly transported to the opening credits of Easy Rider. A young man with the wind in his hair and his life ahead of him. He began to mouth along with the words... 'Ah... those were the days!'

David tutted impatiently. 'Yes, but *who* does it sound like?'

'I've no idea.'

'It's Kate,' said David bluntly.... raising his voice. **'Kate.... is that you?'**

The singing stopped.

'David?' The voice was faint and had a lot of echo, but it was unmistakably Kate's
'Yes.... Kate?... Where are you?'
'We're stuck in the lift!'
'You're what...?'
'We're STUCK.... In the LIFT!'
'Oh bugger! Okay love. You just wait right there. I'm going to get the manager.'

In the lift, Kate looked at Naz. '*"Wait right there"?*' she said, raising an eyebrow. 'Where the hell does he think we're going?'

And they both collapsed into hysterical laughter at the stupidity of their rescuer.

Kate couldn't face going into Leeds with the rest of the crowd that night. David was reluctant to leave her, but his responsibilities as host left him with little choice. He certainly didn't fancy abandoning Rosa and Dominic to the mercy of Jim's complete 'sense of direction bypass'. Particularly as they both had early flights in the morning and didn't want to be too late to bed. He wondered briefly about putting all three presenters in a taxi and having a night off himself, but he still wasn't sure he could trust that they'd get back okay.

'I really don't like the idea of leaving you,' he dithered, standing in her bedroom doorway.

She looked so small tonight and she had that glazed, washed-out look he'd seen so many times when he'd been drafted in to deal with the psychological aftermath of some awful natural or man-made disaster.

She was sitting on the edge of the bed, her shoulders drooping. 'It's okay,' she said. 'I really *am* fine. I think I just need an early night.'

'Can I order you something to eat?'

'No,' she shook her head. 'I'll sort it. I'm not very hungry at the moment, to be honest.'

'God Kate... I wish you'd let me take care of you, for once.'

Wearily, she stood up. 'David... I'm just so grateful that you found us. I hope we didn't traumatise you too much with our singing...' she managed a smile.

'Yeah... what *was* the story with that?'

'Oh...' she laughed. 'I was just doing it to humour the kid... she said it was something her grandmother used to do with her when she was little... It was quite funny.... 'Born to be Wild' with gestures.... A cross between 'Swing Low Sweet Chariot' and British Sign language. Maybe I'll teach it to you some day. It passed the time, at least. You run out of things to do in a lift after the first few minutes, I can tell you!'

David grinned cheekily. '*Some* people might have come up with more interesting things to do. Particularly with a little cracker like that!'

Kate tutted. '*You,* sir, have got a *very* dirty mind.'

'Oh God, yes!' his smile faded. 'Speaking of which, Jim has his eye on you!'

'Oh, please tell me I just misheard!'

'No... I'm sorry. But I thought I'd better tell you. Forewarned is forearmed, as they say.'

'I'll get my pepper spray at the ready.... Now... go get something to eat. Have a nice evening. And please, give my apologies to everyone.'

The minute he had gone, she opened the mini bar. It was fairly well stocked with a bag of peanuts, and cheap copies of Cheddars, Twix and a Mars Bar. There was also a small bottle of sparkling water and a can of something similar to Lilt, plus a reasonable selection of pre-mixed drinks, a few miniatures, and a couple of half bottles of wine, one white and one red. Everything cost about three times its usual price of course, but it avoided the exposure of venturing down to the bar where there was a strong risk of bumping into, and having to make conversation with, people from the conference. Kate had never been a big drinker either, so, even at mini-bar prices, it wasn't going to cost her too much to get plastered.

She decided to start with one of the pre-mixed G & T's, enjoying the sharp *'psst!'* of the can as she ring-pulled it. Then she headed to the en-suite for a long, slow soak in the bath.

Naz was feeling edgy. It wasn't because of being stuck in the lift. That hadn't scared her at all, though the jobs had stacked up for her while she was missing in action, so she'd had a busy evening, unblocking sinks, finding lost keys for guests and helping to release the gentleman whose call-girl had handcuffed him to the bedpost and fled with his wallet.

'Won't use *that* agency again,' she heard Whitlass muttering under his breath as she went past with the bolt cutters.

Kate had been playing on her mind though. The memory of how terrified she had been. Naz had seen the conference presenters and most of the other UKITT members going out for the night. She'd noticed that Kate wasn't with them, or with any of the small groups who had braved the hotel and were mingling now with the crew of the Starship Enterprise in the bar. She kept picturing her, alone in her room, with that awful fear, and she desperately wanted to go to her, just to make sure she was alright.

It was 9 o'clock when Saskia called her over. 'You finish now?' she asked.

'Yes, just clocking off.'

'Not want to take Club Sandwich to Room 59 then?'

Naz could have kissed her. 'God, yes!' she said. 'That's no problem at all!'

'Is down with Charlie in kitchen.'

'Oh Saskia, thank you... thank you!!!' She couldn't resist. She leaned over the counter and kissed her friend quickly on the cheek.

'Eeurgh!' said Saskia fiercely, pretending to wipe the kiss away with her hanky. 'Too much sex pest. Save for Room 59!'

Kate had almost finished her second can of gin and tonic. She had the mild, warm, buzziness that went with being just slightly tipsy. She realised she'd done what her clients described as 'taking the edge off'. It felt nice. Everything was softer now, the shapes, the sounds, her own body in the scratchy towelling dressing gown with a fraying 'Deluxe Hotels' logo on its lapel.

When she opened the door, Naz looked soft too, standing there with her Club sandwich wrapped in cling film on a tray.

She reached out for it and accidentally touched the hand that had held hers only three hours earlier.

Naz looked determined to come into the room. 'Shall I just put it down here?' she asked, sidestepping Kate like a Bell Girl from some much higher class hotel, and carrying it towards the small desk by the TV set playing silently in the corner. 'It's on the house... I think the boss is hoping you won't file a complaint.... Look, how are you? I've been thinking about you all evening?' She turned to face Kate, her deep brown eyes clouded with concern.

Kate became suddenly very aware of her own nakedness beneath the robe, a sense of shyness, followed, almost immediately by a yearning she had believed herself incapable of.

'I'm fine,' she said. 'I'm just sorry I broke your lift.'

'God theresnoneedtobesorry! Ahcome yarent outwiyamates?'

There it was again, thought Kate, the blurriness, it had moved to her ears now. Though, actually, Naz, who was nervous, had simply fallen back into that strange garbled Yorkshire accent of hers. She saw a hazy look of bewilderment in Kate's eyes, and repeated what she'd just said, in English.

Kate, listening harder this time, figured she'd either been blessed with the gift of tongues or she'd sobered up a little. She decided it was probably the latter. It wasn't as if she'd had *that* much to drink, after all.

'They're not really my mates,' she said sadly.

'I thought Mr Cohen was... The nice gentleman who rescued us from the lift.'

'David?.... I've known him a long time. He was one of my tutors when I did my original psychotherapy training and then I suppose we became closer when he founded the Institute and I became a junior member of the teaching staff. He's not really a friend though. He's my supervisor.'

Naz thought of Tracey, who was *her* supervisor. She'd count her as a friend. And Saskia, who was a kind of unofficial supervisor, at least in the sense that she bossed her around... she was definitely a mate. Not Lucinda though, even though she was more bossy than the other two put together. She was *way* too moody and *much* too far up Whitlass's backside for that.

'Well, he seems pretty fond of you.'

Was he? Kate pondered this. She had always assumed that the affection went one way. She paid David for her monthly consultations with him, and he provided insight, encouragement and expertise. He had power over her though. At the end of the day he was there to protect the clients and he could shut her down in an instant if he thought she was out of line.... Guiltily, she regretted not telling him about the texts. She should have flagged it up with him at least, and arranged a time to talk about the problem. She told herself she'd do it as soon as she saw him tomorrow.

Naz noticed that she was distracted. 'Well, anyway, she said. 'I suppose I'd better leave you in peace.' She didn't want to go, but she didn't want to outstay her welcome.

Kate didn't want her to go either.

'I guess you have to get back to work...' she said, tentatively.

'No, I'm finished now for tonight.'

'Well....' She'd seen people do this on the TV... in films... read it in books... People did it all the time... Meeting people, feeling attracted to them... How hard could it be? ... She took a run at it. 'Well, if you're off duty now, would you like to stay and have a drink with me?'

Naz looked into Kate's eyes, checking first, for the genuineness of the invitation... whether it was real, or just some polite gesture. And when she saw that it was real, gauging, as she always did in these circumstances, the signs of how much Kate had had to drink. Where was she on the drunk/sober spectrum? She'd seen the far end of that spectrum too many times in her mother and she could barely tolerate it now. It was something in the eyes that changed first, even before the speech began to slur. Kate wasn't at that stage yet, but she didn't look very far off it either. If she had another drink now, Naz wondered, would it tip her over the edge?

It was as if Kate saw her dilemma. 'This is my last one,' she said, shaking the last couple of inches in the can. 'I have to be careful. Two G&T's and I'm anybody's.'

No sooner were the words out of her mouth than she realised exactly what she'd said.

She felt herself blushing.

Naz smiled, reassured on all counts. 'Have you got a Bacardi and Coke?' she asked.

Kate peered into the tiny fridge. It was nice to feel the cool air on her face.

'White rum and cola,' she reported.

'Well... That's as close as we get to brands at Horton Hill.'

Perched on the edge of Kate's bed, with half the Club Sandwich in one hand and her drink in the other, Naz found that she felt strangely at peace. She knew that most people wouldn't. They'd find Kate's lack of conversation difficult – stressful even. They'd think she was judging them (which she probably was). And they'd be preoccupied with wondering how this was all going to work out... what they were going to get out of it... and whether it would be worth the effort.

But Naz was starting to get the measure of Kate now. She knew that the brittleness was just a wall she put up to protect herself. And the lack of conversation was just a kind of natural reticence, a belief - probably true - that people tend not to be interested very much in anything other than their own views, their own joys and their own problems.

The silence felt good to Naz anyway. It reminded her of her grandmother, seated quietly in front of the Buddha in her ramshackle Victorian conservatory, a single tea light flickering, morning and night. She had found some kind of inner peace there after her turbulent years of sex and drugs and rock 'n roll, and her sadness for the daughter who had been the collateral damage of those years crystallized in the prayers she chanted at the start and at the finish..

Sabbe Satta Sukhi Hontu... 'May All Beings be Well - May All Beings Be Happy'

Naz wondered if her mother would ever reach that place. From the state she'd been in last time she saw her, she doubted it.

In the room now, she noticed that Kate was having a good sniff at her half of the Club Sandwich before taking a bite.

'I've never had *serious* food poisoning while I've been here,' said Naz, teasing her gently.

'Well, that's something, I suppose.'

They both ate in silence, listening to the sounds outside their room, the distant chatter from the bar, the thud of a door, the metallic clunk of the lift. From outside came the eerie yowling of mating cats.

'David... my supervisor.... has been trying to do a bit of matchmaking for me this weekend,' said Kate, emboldened by the gin.

Naz felt uneasy. She hoped it wasn't that lecherous old git she'd seen perving around Kate earlier.

'That's a co-incidence,' she said. '*My* supervisor tried to get me off with someone last night too.'

'Oh?' It came out sharper than she'd expected. 'I imagine you must have loads of women throwing themselves at you?'.... She'd probably slept with most of them too. Suddenly, Kate saw herself as she imagined Naz must see her. An uptight virgin – at least in the sense of never having slept with a woman before. She remembered seeing her in the breakfast room, talking to the slightly contemptuous girl with long bottle-red hair who seemed to be in charge. How they'd glanced in her direction and laughed... *'Gagging for it,'* she imagined them saying. Probably placing bets on Naz's chances of reeling her in. She thought of how she'd confided in Naz in the lift and wondered how she could have been so stupid. She felt angry with David too, that he should be encouraging her into this kind of sleazy sexual encounter.

Seeing Kate's face change, Naz could have kicked herself. She had no idea why she'd even thought to mention last night really, other than that she was nervous and babbling to cover her shyness.

'I don't,' she said, though that wasn't strictly true. The truth – that she *did* but wasn't generally very interested – would have sounded too arrogant. 'It was one of the bridesmaids,' she stammered, like a kid at school trying to explain some misdemeanour. 'Tracey gave her my room number... But I didn't let her in... I mean, we're not supposed to. It's against the rules... Though I'm the only person who's been sticking to that one, apparently...' She ground to a halt. She could see it was useless. The shutters had come down in Kate's eyes. She wasn't really listening.

'I'm sorry,' she said stiffly. 'I hope you don't mind.... but I'm suddenly feeling very tired.'

Naz felt her heart sink as her last glimmer of hope flickered and died.

'Okay,' she said despondently. 'Thank you for the drink.... and for sharing your sandwich with me.'

'Thank you for your help. I've appreciated it.'

Naz stood up. She wanted to plead with Kate. 'Please let me stay. We don't have to do anything... please....' She didn't say it, of course. It would just have made her sound desperate and needy. Instead, she said, 'I might see you in the morning?'

'Possibly. The meeting doesn't finish till 1pm.'

'Okay. Well, good night then.'

'Yes – goodnight.'

Kate stood to lock the door as she let her out.

Naz cast a wry 'goodnight' in the direction of Saskia as she wove through a group of inebriated Bajorans. One of them appeared to be winking at her, but possibly she was just trying to focus around her prosthetic nose ridges. Either way, Naz pretended she hadn't noticed.

'Hey, was too quick!' Saskia called after her friend.

'Yeah.' Naz shrugged. 'Don't ask!'

Back in her room, she sank wearily onto the bed, running her hands through her hair as she battled with the loneliness threatening to engulf her. She felt grief-stricken and close to tears, like she had in those first awful weeks in the children's home when she was still shell-shocked by her Nan's death and her mother's shambolic and brief reappearance in her life.

The time in the lift, the closeness of Kate, the thought that maybe they might have been able to comfort each other - all that - had led her back to that desolate place.

She didn't have a great track record with women. Her first (massive) crush had been on her social worker. A painful, blushing, tongue-tied adolescent passion that had never stood the faintest hope of being requited and which, she always suspected, had led to her being re-assigned to jaded, middle-aged Mr Soames, who smelt of cigarette smoke and halitosis and, thankfully, never found much time to see anything of her at all.

In her late teens, there had been the lecturer on her 'Catering and Hospitality' Diploma at college. She *had* taken her to bed – several times – for some eye-openingly unfettered and rather kinky sex sessions, before suffering a massive crisis of conscience and quoting the college rule book on 'relations between staff and students' like she'd never actually read it before.

And then, in her early twenties, there was Joanne, Saskia's predecessor at Horton Hill, who had simply moved on (and in) with someone closer to her own age leaving Naz secretly sobbing along to Whitney Houston for weeks and wondering what the hell it was that she kept doing wrong.

In her heart, she was starting to believe she was always going to be unlucky in love.

Because, so far, it had always been the same.... hope followed inexorably by disappointment.

Just to prove it to herself, she pulled her phone out of her pocket and dialled.

'Hey, Baby Girl!' Her mother's voice carried the soft, pseudo-Jamaican lilt that was a sure sign of a new boyfriend on the scene. When she talked like that it was hard to believe that, apart from occasional cheap-flight holidays to Marbella or Amsterdam, she had never ventured far from her native West Yorkshire.

'Hey, Mum. How're you doing?'

'Good... yeah... good...'

She was drunk or stoned or both. Lovers Rock reggae was playing distantly, maybe in the next room. Of course, it was Saturday night. There was probably a party going on. The music blasted louder suddenly, accompanied by a man's deep voice murmuring something that sounded like a question.

'It's nobody, Baby,' said her mother to him in reply.

The music quietened again with the click of the door.

'Precious... I gotta...'

'It's okay Mum.'

'I'm sorry. We'll talk soon... yeah?'

'It's okay.'

'I got people round... yah know.'

'No worries Mum. I'm sorry to disturb you.'

'Goodnight Baby.'

'Night Mum.'

The line went dead.

'I love you,' said Naz into the emptiness.

At 4.30am Kate was awakened by another text from the client.

It read: 'What we did was really bad. I feel so used.'

Kate wondered who the 'we' was, and what they had done. She wondered if the client was ok too, and whether she should respond or not. She decided against it in the end. But it's hard to get back to sleep after reading something like that.

Naz woke up about 4.30 too.

She thought instantly of Kate - the way her hair had curled over the collar of the cheap hotel dressing gown. The fine cheekbones, long neck, smooth legs, slight swell of breasts, barely glimpsed as Kate had felt her looking and pulled the lapels of the gown closer even as she'd realised she was doing it and looked away. She remembered the freshly bathed smell of her.... The Horton Hill soap that was supposed to be Baylis and Harding but wasn't.

She wondered if Kate had managed to sleep after the terror of the lift, and the memories it had so obviously stirred in her. Whatever had happened in the past, Naz could see that it was ruining her life. And when she thought about that, it made her want to cry.

Then she thought of her one-time friend Jess, the tall, blonde car mechanic who had taken her under her wing when she first ventured onto the Leeds Gay Scene at seventeen.

Jess was a legend in her own time.

Could get any woman she wanted.

Naz had seen her in action on many occasions. She'd tried to analyse how she did it. She wasn't particularly good looking. She wasn't even particularly nice when you got to know her either – though Naz wondered if that secretly worked in her favour.

One day, when they'd been kicking around, bored, in the bar, she'd asked Jess what her secret was, and for once she got an honest answer.

'You gotta believe you can,' said Jess. 'If you believe you can – you've already got 'em.'

Naz wondered how you went about believing you could when you didn't.

And then she thought, maybe, if she *acted* like she did. Maybe, just maybe, that might work almost as well.

She wondered what someone with Jess's kind of confidence would do and she figured they wouldn't just give up at the first hurdle.

Then she thought about Kate. How shy she was. How she kept distant from people. Organised things and wrote about life from the sidelines. And suddenly she knew what her best shot was.

Hoping against hope that she'd got it right, she dug out the Horton Hill headed paper and a pen she'd squirreled away in her desk drawer – wrote Staff Quarters Room 5 above the address and added her mobile phone number below it. Then she sat chewing the end of the pen, wondering what someone who believed they could, would write.

At breakfast, Kate spoke to David about the texts.

'It's this fairly new client,' she said. 'She seemed to be settling in okay, but since her last session she's been texting in the night. Weird stuff, about how she's done something awful and she's really struggling with it. Stuff like that.'

David felt concerned. Kate was usually very self sufficient as a therapist. A bit too much so, if he was honest. There had certainly been times when she could have done with emergency support and she hadn't asked for it. So either this was really freaking her out or she'd learned her lesson from not asking for help last time. He hoped it was the latter, though her expression suggested that she was actually pretty freaked out by it all too.

'Have you responded?' he asked.

'I waited till morning each time. And then I've just texted back to say that she should try not to worry and we can talk about it at our next session.'

It was a text book response... just what he'd expect from his star pupil.

'Which is when?'

'Tomorrow.'

'Okay.... And you've no idea what it's about.'

'Not an inkling!'

'What's the presenting issue?'

'Domestic abuse. She was referred to me from the refuge. Her husband was really violent. She packed a bag and got out while he was at work one day. She had it all worked out in advance. She's trying to start a new life, but it's hard for her, and she's got some awful memories.'

'Do you think she's at risk?'

'Well. *That's* always a tough call.... But I think she's covered her tracks pretty well...'

'How about risk to herself... suicide?... self harm?'

'I don't think so. We discussed all that at the first session. I think she'd tell me if she was going down that particular road.'

'No drinking, or drugs... anything that might make her act out of character?'

'Not that I know of.'

David sighed. 'Sounds like you're doing everything you can. Will you let me know how the session goes tomorrow?'

'Yes... absolutely. Things might be clearer then.'

They both looked up as Jim joined them at the table. He was carrying a black coffee and a bowl of porridge on a tray. 'I popped round to your room last night,' he said to Kate. 'To see how you were feeling after your ordeal yesterday. I knocked but you didn't answer, so I assumed you must be asleep. I hope I didn't disturb you.'

'No, not at all.' said Kate, not entirely truthfully. 'I must have been hard on.'

'Probably not the only one!' muttered David under his breath.

Jim looked up sharply from his porridge. 'Sorry DC, I didn't catch that.'

David met the eye of his old friend and held his gaze in an unflinching declaration of war.

'I said... that's very touching Jim, especially after our conversation yesterday afternoon.'

Kate assumed that the letter pushed under her door was the bill. She shoved it into her Filofax and handed a couple of boxes of books and papers to David and Jim, who were keen to avoid her having to use the lift again. All that remained was for her to pack her things. The rooms needed to be vacated by 11am, which would be well into the AGM, so everything needed to go back down to the conference room where she could keep a watchful eye on it.

She felt a bit more back to normal today. She'd survived the lift incident and she hadn't succumbed to temptation with Naz. She even felt better about the texts now she'd spoken about them to David.

Flexing her shoulders to ease the tension there, she dressed, simply but neatly in black cotton trousers and white top and headed down the stairs with her suitcase in one hand and her precious flip chart in the other.

To her embarrassment, she realised that word had spread about the lift. People seemed kinder than usual, thanking her for all her hard work, for finding another venue at such short notice, and for the apparently effortless way the conference had run that year. People who previously had eyed her with suspicion were smiling at her as if they liked her. She hated it. It made her feel nervous and patronised and she was glad when she got to 1pm and it was all over.

David and Jim helped her to carry the boxes out into the lobby.

'Let's take them out to your car,' said Jim.

She shook her head, keen to be alone. 'It's okay. I'm parked miles up the road. I'll bring the car round to the front entrance. It's quiet enough out there now all those Star Trek people have gone.'

'Well, if you're sure....' Jim had just spotted one of the more attractive student members about to leave and he wanted to make sure she had his phone number in case she needed "any help with her PhD".

'That man's got serious problems,' growled David.

Kate watched as Jim handed the girl his card.

'Maybe he's lonely,' she said.

'Well he'd be a damn sight less lonely if he chased women his own age!.... Look, are you sure about the car?

I can give you a hand round with these you know.... Or I can wait here and help you in with them.'

'Truly, David, it's really kind of you, but it's not a problem.'

A mischievous grin came over him.

'Or maybe you'd prefer a bit of help from the Hospitality Assistant,' he suggested with a Benny Hill style wink.

Kate blanked it.

'Or maybe not...' he said hastily. 'Anyway, if you don't need me, I'll be off. I promised to call round to see Dan's mum in Sheffield this afternoon on my way home.'

'Oh, that's lovely. She'll be so pleased to see you!' Kate's face softened at the thought of David's partner, Daniel. It was almost two years now since he'd died and she still half expected him to suddenly re-appear by David's side with his lopsided grin and hint of middle-aged spread, cleaning his glasses on the hem of his shirt. She sometimes wondered how David even came close to functioning without him. The two of them had been co-tutors on her therapy training, and she'd seen instantly how devoted they were, as best friends as well as lovers.

She hugged David hard to try to communicate her sympathy to him.

'Thank you for all your help this weekend,' she said.

'I didn't do much.'

'Truly, David... just by being here... you did!... Please drive carefully, won't you.'

'You too!' He found that he wanted to hold her just a little bit longer than he would have done before. He was moved by her still-raw grief for Dan. And he'd realised, through his fury against Jim, just how much he'd come to love her. He wished he could find a way to help her trust the world more. Lighten up. Maybe come out from behind that wall she seemed to have built around herself. It was only in recent years that he'd come to truly understand that kind of wall. It was something he would barely have recognised in his youth.... Something he'd worked with in his clients but never needed in himself. And then the doctors had told him that Dan was going to die, and steadily, day by painful day, he'd constructed a wall of his own, retreated inside it, and slammed the door.

The car was on bricks when Kate got back to it.

Wearily, she phoned Green Flag. They told her they'd be about two hours.

She trudged back to the hotel, where she'd said she would go to wait.

The frosty faced receptionist looked up from filing her nails as Kate entered the lobby.

'Shall I get one of the lads to help you out with your boxes?' she asked.

'Oh, thank you, but no... my car's been vandalised. I'm going to have to wait for the Green Flag man.'

'It would have been safer in the car park. We've got CCTV there. Mind you. It doesn't stop 'em. They just wear hoodies.'

'There wasn't any room in the car park.'

'No.... we've been very busy...' she stopped, mid-sentence, head cocked, listening raptly to the voice that came out of the slightly ajar door of the manager's office.

'Gladys.... Get us a coffee will you?'

She giggled. 'He never *can* remember my name,' she said, as if this were the cutest trait in the world. 'Would you like me to get you a drink too? For while you're waiting?'

'Oh... yes... thank you. A cup of tea would be lovely. That's very kind.'

'We aim to please at Horton Hill.' Lucinda's smile transformed her face. She looked ten years younger. She sounded happy.

My God, thought Kate. *The poor woman's in love with Whitlass – that thug in a suit who struts around the place like he's manager of the Savoy.* She felt sorry for her - particularly as anyone could see that the man was besotted with the stroppy maroon-haired hospitality manager, who held him in clear and unmitigated contempt.

Sinking down to wait on one of the very low and slightly ripped chairs in the lobby, she figured she might as well have a look at the bill while Lucinda was getting the drinks. She took the envelope out of her Filofax and opened it. Then she stared, disorientated, at the slightly child-like handwriting of what was obviously not a bill at all, but a letter.

Dear Kate,
I hope you don't mind me writing to you. It's just that I think you're the most beautiful woman I've ever set eyes on, and I don't want you to leave here without me telling you that.
I know you think I'm just some stupid chancer. It's the baseball cap. It gives the wrong impression. Tracey got it for me as a joke for my Birthday and I don't like to offend her by not wearing it.
I don't just sleep around with all and sundry though. I don't see the point in that.

And I'm not just some loser who's going to be stuck in this place all my life. I'm good at my job and I can move to something better.
I thought maybe, if you'd like, I could have a day off sometime and come to London and take you out for lunch somewhere nice. So we can get to know each other a bit better and see how we get on.
It's just a thought. But if you'd like it, I'd like that very much.
Even if you just throw this letter in the bin, I'll always be glad that I met you.
Yours truly
P. Nazzaro (Naz)

Kate felt her heart rate slowly increasing, like a piston, accelerating, even as she smiled at the quaint and rather old fashioned phrasing of the letter (did kids these days really use terms like 'all and sundry'?). She felt heat flooding and rising up her throat and into her cheeks. It felt almost like the panic she had felt in the lift. She folded the letter and put it back in its envelope.

'Is Naz around?' she asked Lucinda when she came back, humming to herself and pushing a trolley like the ones they used to have at school dinners. It held a tray with a pot of tea and milk and sugar for her, and a similar one with a tall coffee pot and a plateful of chocolate HobNobs for the boss.

'No, she's gone t't'Cash 'n Carry 'n Plumbase. Your lot pulled a washbasin off t'wall and ate all t'Garibaldi's.'

'Gosh,' said Kate ironically. 'I never knew we were so wild.'

'It's allus quiet ones as t'wurst,' said the receptionist. 'Would you like a biscuit with that?'

'No... thank you.' Kate took her tray. 'This is lovely. It's very kind of you.'

She sat, and waited, drinking her tea and glancing at her watch from time to time.

The afternoon dragged as she battled with herself.

Finally, at 3pm, she opened the letter again and hunted in her shoulder bag for her mobile.

'Thank you, Naz,' she texted. 'Lunch sometime would be nice. Regards Kate F.'

Her thumb hovered over 'send' for what seemed like an eternity before she pressed the key and watched the message disappear from the screen.

The response bounced back so quickly, she wondered if Naz had already had it saved in 'drafts'.

':0)' she read. 'Sunday? 12.15? Kings X? xxx Naz.'

Kate stared at the reply. She wanted to type *'Too soon!'*

Instead, she found herself carefully spelling out. 'Thank you. That would be lovely.'

Monday teatime, Kate phoned David.

'I need to arrange an emergency supervision,' she said.

'Do you need me in person, or will the phone do?'

'Phone's fine.'

'I've got time now, if that's any good.'

It was a relief actually.

'It's "The Client",' said Kate, pacing, as she always did when she was on the phone.

'Okay?' David heard the apprehension in his own voice.

'She came for her session today...' It was an anxious pacing, like a caged animal... across the hallway, where the phone base unit was plugged... into the sitting room.... looking out of the window at the trees, the cars parked on the road outside.. people coming home from work...

David heard her journey... the soft shuffle of her feet on the carpet, the creak of the door that needed oiling. Now he could hear a bird singing outside her window. He tried to identify it. Dan would have been able to, but he'd never shared his lover's passion for birds.

'Did you manage to talk to her about the texts?'

'No... She wasn't well. She'd come on the bus. Arrived about five minutes late and asked if she could lie down. She said she was starting with a migraine. She had some tablets with her, and she took those with some water. She said she felt sick, had coloured, zigzag lights at the edge of her vision, couldn't see properly. I asked if it was something that happened often, and she said it was fairly common on the day before her period.'

'Okay....?' the apprehension was deepening.

'She lay down for a while on the sofa and she seemed to fall asleep. It felt a bit strange just sitting there watching her, so I came into the sitting room where I could hear her when she woke up.'

'How long was she asleep for?'

'About half an hour.... It was about twenty to eleven when I heard her stirring. I was getting worried, because I had another client at twelve thirty. I went straight through to her and she said she was still feeling bad.... She didn't *look* great to be honest.'

'So, what did you do?'

She didn't answer immediately.

'What would *you* have done?'

He heard the anxiety in her voice. The fear that she'd got it wrong and he'd be cross with her – or disappointed.

'I don't know,' he said honestly.

'I drove her home,' she said.

'And just dropped her outside?'

'Is that what I should have done?'

'It would have been the safest option.'

'I was worried that she might pass out or something. She said she felt dizzy and couldn't see straight. I asked if she wanted me to take her to the doctors, or even phone an ambulance. But she said it wasn't that serious. It would just pass. It always did. She just needed to lie down.... She said she was wondering if her blood sugar was low. So she went up to her bedroom and I made her a cup of tea and a sandwich and I took them up to her...'

'Into her bedroom?'.... *Oh shit!*

'Yes... Have I been an idiot?'

'No Kate, you haven't, you've responded humanely to a client in distress... I probably would have done the same, in the same circumstances...' *But with a client who had been texting in the night? And with a potentially violent partner? Shouldn't she have been more careful?*

'How was she when you took the stuff up to her room?' he asked.

'She seemed woozy. I encouraged her to have a drink of the tea and she reassured me that she'd be okay. Said she'd see me next week usual time. She thanked me for taking her home.'

'So you just headed back to your place?'

'Yes. I had to get back for the twelve thirty client.'

'Jesus... she's a nightmare, isn't she? *This* one!'

Kate was pacing again. He heard her... out of the sitting room, down the hallway, into the echoing space of the kitchen, where the cushionfloor sucked at her feet as she walked.

'Do you think she's playing me?'

'Truly?... Kate, I don't know... We just don't have enough of her history to make any sense of this...' He'd been doodling on the message pad beside the phone. Now he scribbled through the image he'd created there – a woman propped against pillows smiling. He wished he could scribble out the suspicion that had inspired it, but he couldn't. 'But be careful, please. If she contacts you in any way... in any way at all, before next week's session, you must phone me immediately... Okay?'

'Okay. Thank you.'

'Are you alright?'

Kate shook herself. She didn't *feel* alright. She felt frightened.

'I'm fine,' she said, forcing a smile into her voice. 'Thanks for being there David, Is it okay if I pay you for this session when I see you next?'

God, she was always *so* correct! He smiled, thinking of her utter dedication to getting it right. 'Don't be daft,' he said warmly. 'We've only been on the phone five minutes. And don't worry. You haven't done anything wrong. It's all going to be fine. I'm sure.'

But he was speed-dialling his own supervisor the minute he'd hung up the call.

Naz had only happy memories of London. As the train pulled into Kings Cross, she remembered day trips with her Nan to art exhibitions at the Tate or Royal Academy and concerts in iconic venues like The Shepherd's Bush Empire and The Royal Festival Hill. And then there were the boisterous, garlic-heavy meals at Great Uncle Giuseppe's restaurant on the Fulham Rd, with copious amounts of Chianti (full strength for the adults and watered down for Naz and her cousins) that never seemed to make anyone drunk like it would do at home with mum – just huggy and full of warmth and laughter and gentle affectionate teasing.

The restaurant was gone – burnt down in a fire that may, or may not, have been accidental. And the family were more or less gone now too, dispersing with the fire that sent the great-cousins into a spiral of recriminations and feuding that shattered the family and left Naz, isolated in Leeds at the best of times, alone.

She wished they were still there. She could have taken Kate to the restaurant and shown her that she had a family to be proud of. She knew the boys would have flirted outrageously with her 'Beautiful Friend' and the women would have done their best to 'fatten her up' on pasta and tiramisu. She couldn't imagine telling them that Kate was a 'girlfriend'. Not with the crucifix hanging on the wall and the statue of the Virgin Mary on the fireplace and her great-cousins crossing themselves all over the place. Though goodness knows, Nan had been a 'right little trollop' in her youth and none of them ever seemed to have held that against her.

Anyway, they were gone. There wasn't anything Naz could do about it. And she was determined not to let anything spoil her happiness today.

Stepping into the nasal hubbub of train announcements, chattering voices, and the jerky thrum of wheelie-cases being dragged along the platform, Naz was excited and nervous all at the same time at the prospect of being re-united with Kate.

She'd dressed carefully and after lots of consultation with Saskia, in thin, blue skinny jeans, sandals, and a white cotton top that was V-necked and a little bit more feminine than her usual stuff. She hadn't wanted to look like she was wearing her work uniform, and she'd wanted to be comfortable, but she needed to be smart enough to get into any restaurant Kate might fancy. Secretly, she hoped it wouldn't be *too* posh though, as she only had a hundred pounds to play with on her pay-as-you-go credit card and after her spontaneous big gesture in the letter, she didn't want to look like a total div by having to ask Kate to contribute.

Her anxiety mounted as she got closer to the barriers. She'd been so busy planning how to get here, it had never occurred to her till now that Kate might simply stand her up, leaving her with a whole day to kick her heels alone in London before she could return home in shame to Tracey's 'I told you so's and a volley of Saskia's unrepeatable expletives about 'Stuck up Tango Bitch,' on her behalf.

But they saw each other simultaneously, and their faces lit up in a mutual grateful smile of recognition as they waved across the station concourse.

Naz was rewarded for her long journey by a kiss on the cheek. She tried to kiss Kate back, but she had already dodged out of reach.

'The train was exactly on time,' said Kate, as if she were making conversation with a business colleague who had just turned up for a meeting.

'Yes, it was a good journey.' And Kate was so beautiful. Her hair shone. Her eyes sparkled. The soft, grey blouse she was wearing swooped loosely to just below her hips, and her cropped white trousers teamed with pale grey sandals showed off her tanned calves perfectly.

'I thought it would be best for *you* to choose where to eat,' said Naz, with fingers metaphorically crossed. '... As you live here and I don't.'

Kate smiled. 'What time do you have to get back?'

'I've booked the 8pm train, but I can go off and entertain myself after lunch if you've got things to do.' That was the problem with cheap tickets. You always had to specify the train. It didn't give any leeway for running out of conversation after the first half hour. Now Naz came to say it, she wondered if she'd overestimated how long she was going to want to be there.

But she was relieved to see that Kate looked okay with it.

'That's nice,' she said. 'I'm free till five-ish, as least. Do you want to eat in town, or would you like to head out closer to my place?'

'Crikey...' That felt like an unfair question. 'Whichever feels best for you.'

'There's a nice Thai restaurant just down the road from my flat.'

The truth was that Kate had decided she was going to sleep with Naz... assuming that Naz still wanted her, of course. It was a fairly dispassionate decision. A bit like when she fixed on her university course and doing therapy training and buying her flat. A logical decision based partly on the fact that she liked Naz, but mostly on the idea that she felt stupid, at almost thirty, for identifying herself as a lesbian, when she'd never, actually, slept with a woman.

It was as simple as that. Or at least *then* it was as simple as that. Naz seemed nice. She was attractive and Kate figured she wouldn't make her feel dirty or stupid or gauche. It was, as some of Kate's younger clients might say, 'A no-brainer.'

The Thai restaurant was cool and quite dark after the brightness of the early August sunshine.

They were greeted by a tiny woman of indeterminate age. She was traditionally dressed in silk that glistened with gold and metallic blue and green threads.

She bowed her head and joined her fingers in an inverted V that instantly reminded Naz again of her Nan in front of the Buddha. Automatically, she returned the greeting...

Namaste – The Holiness in me greets the Holiness in you.

The air was rich with the scent of Thai spice and the gentle hum of contented conversation. Following the waitress, they passed tables filled with people at various stages of Sunday lunch. Silently, she gestured them towards a small round table for two in the corner. It had a crisp white tablecloth set with heavy silver cutlery and a single red carnation in a vase. Sitting, facing out into the room, Naz noticed that there was a giant gold and gem encrusted elephant on a dais in the centre. There were photographs of the Thai Royal family on the walls.

The waitress handed each of them a huge menu in a black leatherette cover.

'Shall I get you some drinks while you choose?' she asked.

Kate was nervous. 'Could you fancy some wine?' she asked Naz.

'Maybe, just a glass.'

'White?'

'Yeah... that's fine by me.'

'Okay.. could we have a half carafe of your house white please?' Kate smiled up at the waitress and Naz noticed how she had automatically taken over, even though this was supposed to be *her* treat.

It was as if Kate had read her mind. 'There's no way I'm letting you pay for this?' she said, firmly. Not after you've had to fork out for a return train ticket to get here.'

'It wasn't expensive,' Naz protested. 'And we agreed that I'd be treating you. That was the deal.'

Kate looked amused. 'You can be stubborn, can't you?' she said, teasing.

'Well, it's a matter of principle!'

Kate didn't respond. Instead she was scanning the menu with the air of someone who already knew it off by heart.

'It's great food here,' she said. 'I sometimes get their takeaways on a Friday or Saturday night as a treat.'

To eat alone in your flat, thought Naz. She could see why Kate got up Tracey's nose. And she was going to pay for this meal if it killed her.

'Do you fancy to share some starters?'

'Yes. That sounds nice. Do you want to choose?'

'Okay.... is there anything you don't like?'

Naz shook her head.

'Great! And for your main course... It's all lovely...'

'I like the look of the Masaman curry.' Naz liked those rustic meals with potatoes. She'd always liked the pasta dish with new potatoes and asparagus that was one of her Nan's specialities.

Looking across the table, she wondered what it was that she found so attractive in women like Kate... buttoned up, respectable looking women with a false air of confidence that always sat so uncomfortably with them. She invariably went for that type, and they'd always broken her heart. It was as if she saw their vulnerability and wanted to take care of them. But it never worked. They always seemed to be focused so much on everyone else's opinion, they never really had the faintest idea what they wanted for themselves.

The waitress returned and poured two small glasses of wine before putting the carafe on the table. She stood with notepad open and pencil poised.

'We'd like to share some starters,' said Kate. ' Khanom Jeeb Pak, Tod Mun and some Som Tum.... Followed by the Gang Masaman with...'

'Prawn,' said Naz.

'And a Yum Gai Tod Mango.... What kind of rice would you like Naz...'

'Jasmine, if they've got it.'

'Any side dishes?'

'No, that's all good for me.'

'That's it then. Thank you.' She closed her menu and handed it back to the waitress, reaching for Naz's to pass on too.

Naz smiled to herself. She could see that Kate was nervous as hell. It made her inclined to forgive the bossiness.

'Cheers!' said Kate, lifting her glass.

'Cheers!'

She noticed that Kate drank quickly.

'I've been dying to know,' she said, topping up her glass. 'What does the 'P' stand for?'

'The P?'

'In P. Nazzaro?'

'Oh, God... Do I have to tell you? It's bloody embarrassing.'

Kate grinned. 'Well, you signed it... Come on... How bad can it be?' she tried to think of names that really wouldn't suit Naz. 'Petula, Petronella, Primrose, Pearl....?'

'Precious,' said Naz, with disgust.
'Well, I think that's pretty!'
'Yeah – pretty ironic, for a kid nobody wanted.'
Kate heard the hurt behind the words and flagged that it was well under control. 'Yes, but seriously. It's a lovely name... Like Precious Ramotswe.'
Naz looked blank.
'You know, "The Number One Ladies Detective Agency".'
'Nope,' said Naz. 'That's not ringing any bells.'
'I'll lend it to you.... So what's wrong with Precious?'
Naz shrugged. 'Nothing really It's just that I've always been teased about it. 'Specially since the 'Lord of the Rings' films came out.
'Oh, God, yes... I can see that.'
Kate instantly pictured the creepy Gollum with his big sad eyes and obsessive longing for the ring. *'My precioussssss'* she intoned, wincing.
'There you go,' said Naz, laughing now at the very bad impression. 'Imagine how many times you need to hear *that* before it stops being funny.'
Kate could see how it would start to grate after a while.
'And Nazzaro?'
'Apparently something to do with going off to the Crusades, but I guess most people have got dodgy ancestors *somewhere* along the line.'
'Oh!' Kate was quite interested in this - though it wasn't actually what she'd meant.
'How did *you* get to be Precious Nazzaro?' she asked
'Well.... Great Grandpapa Nazzaro was an Italian POW during the Second World War, and Great Grandma Dolly was in the Land Army. They fell in love over the turnip fields near Doncaster and they stayed here because Great

Grandma Dolly didn't like hot weather – crazy woman! They had six kids, including my Nan who was a bit of an afterthought. She met my granddad at the Reading Festival in 1973. He said he was one of Genesis's roadies, but I think that was just a line to get her into a bunk up behind the Genesis tour bus.... They never swapped numbers and she never saw him again. My dad's family are from Trinidad. He's a nice guy, but he was seventeen and he couldn't handle Mum. Then his new girlfriend couldn't handle the thought of him having a kid already, so I don't see him very often. He's cool though. He's a mental health nurse. How about you....?'

'Gosh...' Kate was still digesting this whistle-stop history of Naz's family.

She felt quite relieved when the waitress arrived with the starters and gave her a bit of thinking time.

'There's not much to tell,' she said, when they were alone again with their food.

'Well, tell it anyway.' Naz wasn't going to let her off the hook that easily.

'My family have lived in and around North London for generations. Mum and Dad met at the youth group of the chapel they both went to at the time. They got married when Dad was twenty two and Mum was twenty. They tried for ages to have kids, and then just when they'd given up all hope... I came along. By then they'd joined a very evangelical church. I think Mum probably thinks that getting pregnant had something to do with that. They don't know I'm gay of course. I've never told them and they're highly unlikely to have ever read anything I've written on the subject.' She didn't say what was in her heart... That her mother had been a nervous wreck who sought refuge in the uncompromising dogma of a 'Born

Again' Christian faith that utterly rejected Kate's sexuality. And her father, besotted still by the wife he had always seen as "much too good" and "much too pretty" for a guy like him, had gone along with it all simply because it seemed to keep the love of his life happy.

She tried to get the spotlight back on Naz. 'What made you go into the hotel trade?' she asked.

'I fancied the lady on the registration desk at college. I'd gone to sign up for a Residential Care Administration and Management Diploma, but *she* looked like a right old battleaxe, so I changed my mind.'

Kate laughed. 'I can't believe you just said that!'

Naz laughed too, though the version she'd just given wasn't far from the truth.

'Anyway, what made you become a therapist?' she asked.

'I don't know.' This was a lie. 'I guess I just wanted to help people.'

Naz looked dubious. 'My mum went to see a counsellor once,' she said. 'She got her to write a letter to my Nan telling her all the things she'd done wrong and how much it had screwed Mum up and made her into a bad mother herself. Nan cried when she read it. I thought it was a pretty cruel thing to do.'

Kate felt herself rising to the defence of her profession.

'I imagine the counsellor didn't mean for your mum to send it,' she said.

'Well, why write it then?'

'I don't know.... maybe to help her get in touch with her feelings?'

'Oh...' said Naz. 'Right.'

'You sound doubtful.'

Naz shrugged. 'Mum never had any problem getting in touch with her feelings in the first place,' she said. 'It was *dealing* with them that was always the big problem for her... Anyway... These are nice....' She obviously thought it was time to change the subject, and Kate was grateful to be able to focus on the uncontentious issue of the food.

'Yes', she agreed. 'I think they're my favourites.'

'Mine too... I like this place. I'm glad you chose it.'

'Thank you!' Kate's whole face lit up when she smiled. 'If you like it, I'm glad I chose it too.'

'Would you like a coffee, or anything?' Kate asked as Naz followed her into the hallway of her flat.

'Only if *you* do.'

Kate saw the way Naz was looking at her, and her stomach gave a lurch of fear.

'I feel really stupid,' she said.

'You don't need to.' Naz moved closer and cupped Kate's face in her hands.

'I mean... It's a long time since I've done this.'

'It's okay.'

Kate wasn't sure what to do. She felt the softness of Naz's lips, warm against hers. It felt nice... but scary. She struggled with her automatic urge to pull away, and forced herself to respond, feeling a flush of heat deep within, taking her off guard and creating an urgency she had never expected.

She felt her lips parting as Naz ran a hand down her arm. The heat spread and pulsed within her. She stretched.

Naz took her hand.

Kate led her into the bedroom.

She'd tidied up in preparation for this. The room looked welcoming... sun streaming through the window, the bed covers turned back. She wondered if she should put music on. Wasn't that what people did? She'd downloaded some chart music earlier in the week, thinking that Naz might like it, and she fumbled with the docking station on her bedside table now, found 'Stay with Me' and set the rest to 'Shuffle'. Naz waited for her, patiently beside the bed. She reached out and smoothed Kate's hair back from her forehead as she returned into her arms.

'We can just do *this* if you want,' she said, kissing Kate again, softly, on the lips, then on her brow, her forehead.... 'We've got all the time in the world.' Actually, she would have liked that. To just lie on the bed with Kate in that warm, sunny room, lazily kissing, cuddling, seeing where it all might lead... It was something she'd never really had with the women she'd chosen.

Like young lovers... *first* lovers... thought Kate..... finding all this out for themselves, *from* themselves...

She hadn't expected the tears... suddenly surging, choking and overwhelming her. She had expected it to come back in some other way. Not this grief for how it hadn't been.

The music wavered at the edge of her consciousness.

Naz had stopped kissing her... concerned. 'Kate... Are you okay?'

'No, I'm sorry.... Oh God.... I'm so sorry.... I can't do this.'

She half ran to the bathroom. Shutting the door behind her. Pressing her head back against its coolness. Forcing herself to breathe as the tears poured down her face.

Wondering why the hell she'd embarked on this, knowing it would bring all of that back.

At least they hadn't had mobile phones. No Facebook to be humiliated on. Only a crude note passed from desk to sniggering desk, finally confiscated by the teacher, who binned it in disgust before turning back to the board and continuing with the lesson....

Why the fuck was she putting herself through this?

Naz was tapping on the door.

'Kate? Is everything okay. Have I done something to upset you?'

Kate drew a deep breath. 'No... I'm sorry... It's just.... I...'

She swung out of the door and into Naz's arms. She turned her face away in shame.

'I'm so sorry,' she said again.

Naz held her and she didn't attempt to break free. 'It's okay,' she said gently.

Kate shook her head. 'No... no, it's not. I led you on. I had you coming to London. I brought you back here...'

'Well, I didn't just come to get you into bed.'

'Didn't you?' Kate looked small and a bit bewildered.

It made Naz feel like a total creep. 'Of course I didn't,' she said. 'I like you and I wanted to get to know you better. Look... we just had a great meal together... I think we enjoyed ourselves, didn't we?'

Kate nodded, wretchedly.

'And we've got another couple of hours left. We can do anything you like. We can play Scrabble if you want... Have a walk in the park... or just chill...' She hesitated, not wanting to add the next bit, but feeling she had to. 'Or I can leave now and never darken your doors again.... if that's what you want.' Naz held her breath as she waited for Kate's reply. She wasn't sure how she'd handle it if that was what Kate asked of her.

Kate shook her head. 'No,' she said. 'That's not what I want.'

'Well then,' Naz breathed an audible sigh of relief. 'If that's not what you want, we've still got all the time in the world. Come on... let's just go for a walk, eh. Somewhere you know I'll not be able to jump on you.'

The park was loud with children's play.... shrieks of laughter, the metallic creak of the swings, rising high into the azure sky. Off to the left, a group of teenagers were playing football *'Here... here... Mo, you tosspot... here... to me....'* Lovers walked hand in hand, leaning into each other, sharing kisses or just smiling into each other's eyes.

Naz would have liked to have held Kate's hand. She wanted the world to know that this beautiful woman was here with her today. But she knew that Kate would be much too embarrassed to be gay in public. So they walked slowly, close, but not too close, through the rose garden that smelt like Great Grandma Dolly and her too-brief cuddles by the fireside.

'I don't want to talk about it,' said Kate suddenly.

'Okay.' Naz shrugged. She understood that. There were lots of things *she* wouldn't want to talk about either. She grinned mischievously. 'If we don't have to talk, how about I race you to the ice cream van instead?'

'Do you think there's time?' asked Kate, sheepishly, standing, keys in hand, wishing she could have had the courage to do this earlier.

Naz searched her eyes to see if she really meant it this time.

They shone a pretty clear message.

Naz smiled. 'There's time, even if I miss my train!' she said, holding out her hand and leading the way back into the bedroom.

Afterwards they lay, briefly, quietly, in each other's arms. The lowering sun, shining through the branches of the trees outside, cast a soft, lacy, golden pool of light over them.

'Thank you,' said Kate. She could still feel where Naz had been inside her, a kind of almost soreness, an aching for her return. She ran her finger gently down Naz's cheek, over the butterfly tattoo on her wrist. *You've transformed me,* she thought, without daring to say it out loud.

Naz snuggled into her. Nuzzled kisses into her hair. 'You're amazing,' she murmured.

Kate sought out her lips again and kissed them. 'I wish you could just stay with me... here... now.... Freeze time. Miss your train.... Just stay with me here in this perfect moment.'

'...Did that sound too intense?' she asked, fearfully, when Naz was silent.

Naz had been relishing the words, storing them in her heart for the long days before they could be together again. She half jumped as she realised she hadn't replied... hadn't known she needed to.

'God no,' she said hastily. 'I was just thinking the exact same thing.'

It was almost midnight when Naz got back to the main entrance of Horton Hill.

Saskia had her earphones in and was nodding her head in time to the music, singing 'Yo love is Tequila!' along with Sean Paul and Fuse ODG, rather more loudly and certainly a lot less tunefully than she intended, while sipping orange juice laced with a double vodka from the bar.

She took the earphones out the minute she saw Naz. 'So?' she said eagerly. 'Tell all!'

'Oh God Saskia. She's **gorgeous!**'

'Who's gorgeous?' This was Tracey, appearing from the dining room where she'd just finished clearing up after a group of Japanese tourists on a budget tour of 'Romantic Bronte Country.'

Saskia rolled her eyes in Naz's direction. 'Kate, pain-in-arse, but-fuckable Ferrings,' she said.

Tracey looked suitably disgusted.

'Well, I like her!' Naz protested. 'She's really sweet and nice underneath it all.'

'Oooooh!' Saskia clasped her hands over her heart. 'Naz luuuurves Kate.'

'Oh pur-lease tell me it isn't true.' Tracey shook her head in despair.

Naz laughed, taking their teasing in good part. 'I'm off to bed,' she said. 'And you'll both be getting a thick ear in the morning if you keep on disrespecting my girlfriend.'

Then she headed happily out in the direction of the staff block, pursued by a chorus of *'Oooooh's* from her friends.

Kate had been for her morning run and was showered and sitting in the kitchen with toast, marmalade and her second cup of coffee when Naz's text came through. 'Hi Gorgeous!' it read. 'Been dreaming of you all night.'

Kate smiled as she read it. She'd never received a text like that before. It felt nice - like she mattered to someone.

She was trying to think of something suitably light-hearted to text back when the door bell distracted her with a fit of buzzing like a nest-full of angry hornets.

'Okay... okay!' she muttered, putting her toast down. 'I'm coming. Keep your hair on.'

The feeling of anxiety lagged slightly behind her irritation, but it was at full force by the time she reached the door. It was too early for Mormons.... slightly too early even for a parcel delivery.... She opened the door and looked out quizzically at the couple standing on her doorstep.

'Kathryn Ferrings?' The man was tall, angular and grey-blonde, possibly heading up for his fifties, with a white striped button-down shirt and very new looking designer jeans in traditional indigo. The woman beside him was Asian, a bit younger and dressed in a navy blue trouser suit and white blouse. She had high heels that made her look slightly taller than she was, but she still only came up to her companion's shoulder. Kate was pretty sure she'd never set eyes on either of them before.

'Yes?' she said, managing to make it sound like an answer and a question all in one.

'I'm DS Laclan and this is my colleague DS Shah....' They flashed their IDs in unison and so quickly they could have been library cards for all the chance Kate had of reading them.

'We're investigating a suspicious death at Number 5, Jarald Street. A woman by the name of Lydia Dryer.' DS Shah had picked up seamlessly where her partner left off. She noticed that Kate's hands flew to her mouth when she mentioned the address and stayed there as she added the name into the mix. Something smelt distinctly 'off' about this case. Not least because they'd had an anonymous tip-off about it. Anonymous letters were not unusual at the station. They came for all kinds of reasons; fear of reprisals at one end of the scale and pure (if it could be called that) malicious intent at the other. But they didn't generally come about deaths that hadn't made it onto the news and which, to all intents and purposes, looked like suicide. 'May we come in?' she asked.

'Yes... yes... of course.' Kate led them into her sitting room. The morning sun was just starting to light the far wall, where she'd hung a fiery Whistler print of the Thames at dawn. It had been a present to herself when she passed her psychotherapy registration. Apart from her best friend Sue who had sent a teddy bear wearing a cap and gown and clutching a diploma, no-one else had seen fit to mark the occasion. 'Can I get you a drink of anything?'

'No,' they both shook their heads as if she'd just offered them a bribe.

They sat, side by side on the sofa; his long legs stretched out under the coffee table in front of him, hers bent at the knee and tucked back neatly.

Kate stared at them miserably. She was re-running the case of the client from Jarald Street in her head. The presenting issue; the middle-of-the-night texts; the migraine on Monday... Taking her home, and leaving her there, all against her better judgment. Lydia Dryer.... the "difficult client". The one she'd talked to David about. The one who should have been seeing her that morning, at ten, for her usual appointment.

'When?' asked Kate.

'Last Monday.... we think.... The owner of the property didn't find the body till yesterday.'

DS Shah – Jamila to her friends - thought of the traumatised landlady, Nancy Morgan (aged 80), who had called 999. She'd interviewed Nancy and pictured her, returning home from her visit to the daughter in Southsea she rarely saw. In her imagination she had seen the taxi draw away as Nancy unlocked the door. It was just on the Yale, which meant that Lydia must be in. Jamila felt the loneliness of the panelled hallway. Noticed the smell the elderly lady had attributed at first to a problem with the drains. Kate Ferrings was a trauma counsellor. She worked with the police. She knew about such things. Jamila knew that Kate was picturing it too, even without Nancy's statement. She saw her swallow to try to clear the sudden nausea that rose, unbidden, to her throat, as her hand returned to her mouth. 'I shouldn't have left her.' Kate looked stricken. 'This is my fault. I could see that she was ill and I never even phoned her GP.'

Shah and Laclan exchanged glances. They were deciding who should speak next.

'Ms Dryer didn't die of natural causes,' said Laclan, as Jamila went back into the picture, walking with the old lady, through her house, up the stairs, quickly, despite the arthritis crackling in her knees, to the rooms she had let to Lydia Dryer, who had touched her heart, reminding her of herself, fifty years ago, fleeing from a violent husband, who had sworn that he would kill her. She saw Nancy now in her mind's eye, finding the door ajar and touching it gently, then peeping in. Hearing a quiet buzzing over the silence. Knowing, deep inside, that something was dreadfully wrong. Then her wrinkled hand, dotted with age spots, flying to her mouth just as Kate's had done.

Jamila watched the colour drain from the therapist's face.

She had done her homework about Kate.... Kathryn Ferrings; Psychotherapist and Trauma Specialist. Bright young thing. An approved Trauma counsellor with The Met, no less. Jamila knew people who had been to see her. They were usually in a pretty bad way by the time *that* happened. Nobody in the police wanted to look soft, though they dealt on a daily basis with things no-one should ever be asked to see. But Kate had a good reputation. She didn't mess around being 'touchy feely'. Didn't look sympathetic, with her head on one side and make 'Uhhuh,' noises. Didn't wear hippy dippy clothes. Didn't, in fact, piss her clients off at all. She got people back on their feet and they respected her for it. Kate Ferrings was as close as a civilian freelancer could get to being 'One of our own'. So it interested Jamila that someone had sent an anonymous note with a North London postmark stating that a black Citroen C1 (complete with full registration number) had parked in the Pay and Display car park at the end of Jarald Street at 11am on the morning of Monday 28th July, and that a woman clearly fitting Kate's description had entered the premises with the new lodger and had emerged around half an hour later looking "agitated" without her.

'How then?' asked Kate, despite the part of her that didn't want to know. 'How did she die?'

'I'm afraid we're not at liberty to tell you that at the moment,' said Laclan.

Suicide then.... Or hunted down and battered to death by that bastard of a husband. Kate remembered David asking if she thought Lydia was at risk. And she knew now that she must have missed something. It was every therapist's worst nightmare and constant threat. Depression and/or domestic abuse could escalate so quickly. All it needed was too much to drink, a bad day at the office, or a paranoid suspicion of infidelity.... All those, and more, had been factors in Lydia's story. And all Kate could think was that she should have played safe. She should have seen the texts as a warning sign. She should have phoned the GP.

'What was your relationship with Lydia Dryer?' asked Laclan.

'I was her.... I'm sorry, I need to make a phone call,' said Kate. 'I need to check with my supervisor how much I'm allowed to say.'

'The woman's dead,' said Laclan. 'You need to tell us anything you know that helps us find out what happened.'

DS Shah put her hand on his arm and felt a tremor go through him as if she had given him the mildest of electric shocks. 'Let her get permission from her supervisor,' she said.

They didn't insist on it, but somehow Kate felt she needed to be as transparent as possible. She brought her mobile phone into the sitting room, taking some comfort from the sight of Naz's message still on the screen before she went to David's number, switching to loudspeaker as she called.

She hoped David would answer. He didn't always, preferring to leave the phone on silent and deal with calls at his convenience. Today though, he answered at the second ring.

'Oh Kate, thank goodness!' his voice boomed across the room. 'I was just going to phone you. I've been dealing with a backlog of Institute letters and I've just come across one posted on the 25th. I'm really sorry Kate and I'm sure this is all just a storm in a tea cup... but it's a request to file a formal complaint against you. It's from a client called Lydia Dryer. Is this the one we had the emergency supervision about last Monday?'

Naz managed to stay optimistic until lunchtime; telling herself that Kate was busy, had clients, may not have got her text.... She sent another one: 'Hey, beautiful! How about texting your girlfriend?'
There were a couple of PPI's and 'We can help you claim for your accident' spams that set her heart racing as they beeped, then crashed her back into dejection when she read them.
By mid-afternoon, a dark mood had begun to build within her. She couldn't quite formulate it. But it was something about all the ways the women in her life had let her down.

At 9pm, as she moped around the lobby emptying the waste bins there, she recognised the mood as depression. Tracey saw the edginess in her immediately as she turned the corner from the function room where she'd been setting up for a kiddies' birthday party the following afternoon.
'Any news?' she asked.
There was no sign of Naz's trademark grin that night. 'News?' she muttered bitterly. 'Yeah... Tomorrow's headlines... "P. Nazzaro – Officially the World's Biggest Loser"'

Tracey's heart went out to her. She loved Naz to bits. She had so much to give. If only she would stop continually falling for the wrong women.

'Oh love... I'm sorry. It's her loss you know.'

'Yeah, yeah!'

'Look, why don't you knock off early. I'll cover for you. You're tired. Get yourself a good night's sleep. Things always look better in the morning. Trust me, I've dated more than my fair share of bastards over the years.'

'Thanks T.'

'You're welcome. Just don't have that face on you when I see you in the morning. Okay?'

It was a moment of madness. The van was parked for the night behind the kitchens. The key was dangling in its usual place just inside the rear loading door.

Charlie and Max, the head chef, were at the far end of the kitchen clearing up.

No-one saw her as she unlooped the key from its hook.

Then she was off into town in what was, technically, a stolen Horton Hill van.

The jukebox was playing 'These Girls Ain't Loyal', as Naz walked into the bar. She allowed herself a bitter laugh as she heard it.

It was a typically quiet Monday night crowd. A smattering of lipstick lesbians, not easily discernible from the 'here with my best gay friend' hetero girls with white wine and a lot of cleavage... A few gay guys, most of them pretty camp.... one or two butch types – male and female.... And Jess, sitting on her usual barstool hunched over the dregs of a pint, looking half-cut.

'Hey!' she said, as Naz joined her. 'Haven't *you* grown up!' She drained her glass. 'Me... on the other hand.... *I've* just grown older.'

She wasn't joking. In the five years since Naz had seen her, she had aged dramatically. Her hair was heavily streaked with grey. Her arms, with their tattoos of a lion (on the left) and a Cross of Saint George (on the right) were leathery. And there was a distinct roll of fat around her waist, clearly visible under the white T-shirt that was just that little bit too tight for her.

'Are you gonna buy me a drink?' she asked.

The barmaid was blonde, pierced and indifferent. Naz didn't remember her from before. She didn't smile at her, so she didn't get a smile back. She doubted whether she would have done anyway.

'Mardy cow!' Jess commented when she was out of earshot. 'It's not t'same since Cynth left.'

Cynth had been a kind of on-off girlfriend of Jess's and Jess had treated her like dirt, despite, or maybe because it was pretty plain that Cynth loved her. Naz wondered if she'd gone because she just couldn't bear it anymore.

'Any road.... What brings *you* back here?'

Naz wasn't sure. She grabbed the Rum and Coke as soon as the barmaid put it down in front of her. She'd asked for a double-shot. She had every intention of getting wasted.

Her phone rang and she almost dropped it on the floor in her eagerness to answer it, then she put it down on the bar as Tracey's name flashed urgently on the screen.

Jess leaned over to look. 'Girlfriend?' she asked.
'Boss.'
'S'bloody late for your boss to be phoning.'
'Not when we've just nicked the works' van.'

Jess spluttered into her pint. 'You allus used to be such a good girl too!'

'Not anymore.'

The voice mail icon took a long time to appear on the screen. Naz imagined the message would be very long, very loud, and very unrepeatable. She decided not to listen to it.

'Same again,' she said to the barmaid.

'You'll be getting your s'en rat-arsed!' said Jess, looking at her appraisingly.

'Yeah,' said Naz. 'That's the idea.'

And she did. Somewhere in the region of her fifth rum and Coke, the phone rang again and Kate's name flashed up on the screen.

Jess saw Naz's face change. 'Now... *that's* the girlfriend!' she said, with utter certainty.

Everything in Naz screamed that she should answer it. But she didn't. 'Ex.' She said, rejecting the call.

Jess raised an eyebrow, taking an e-cig out of her pocket and dragging on it before looking at it in disgust. 'Chuffin' smoking ban,' she said. 'Got us all puffin' on plastic dummies. Four refreshing fruit flavours and not one of 'em with an ounce of bang!'

'Fancy to go outside for the real thing?' asked Naz.

'Wondered how long it'd take for you to ask that,' said Jess.

The yard behind the bar was flagged and weed choked and slippery with old burger cartons and condoms from the lads. There was a filthy, boarded up window with a mossy stone sill that felt damp against Naz's hands as she gripped it. A faint smell of urine was overpowered by rotting food in the overflowing industrial bins that hid them from the people walking by in the alleyway beyond.

Jess's hands were rough. Her fingers groped and shoved too hard and too fast. Her tongue tasted of beer as it exploded into Naz's mouth. She wondered quite *when* she was going to be sick. She hoped it would be after it was all over.

Jess wiped her hands on Naz's jeans before she lit her cigarette. 'Allus knew I'd have you in the end,' she said, taking a long, hard drag.

Naz watched the glowing tip fading from view as Jess headed off down the alley for her last bus home. And then, finally, she threw up violently behind the bins.

Kate stared at her phone for a long time after Naz rejected her call. At first, she thought it must just have been an inconvenient moment and that she would phone back.

And when she didn't, Kate had no idea at all of what to do next.

It had been a terrible day. First, the news of Lydia's death and the flood of guilt and soul-searching *that* had unleashed; then the call to David and his bombshell about the complaint.

The rest had seemed to just follow naturally. It was, she knew, the right thing to do... Accompanying the police to the station, giving a statement, fingerprints, DNA samples 'for elimination purposes'. Signing her notes on Lydia over to the police. She feared their judgment. Assumed they must be thinking that she had failed this client in some way. She could see that DS Shah was sympathetic and mildly suspicious. Laclan was unreadable. He seemed to be a shy man, despite his rather dapper dress-sense. Not a typical 'copper' at all.

She had felt exhausted when she finally got home. There had been clients to contact to 'explain' her hasty texts to them that morning cancelling their sessions. ('I'm so sorry, there was an emergency... Yes, everything's fine... thank you for asking... Is it possible for us to re-arrange?'). A call to David, who had been asked to take the letter to the police station and give a statement and who kept apologising for 'landing her in it', even though he'd done absolutely nothing wrong. A cheery text to Sue, asking how she was doing and how about catching up on the phone sometime later in the week? Then her regular call to her parents. ('Yes, it's been a busy day. Nothing out of the ordinary. How are you and Dad....?'). And it was almost bedtime before she forced herself to eat a couple of slices of toast that seemed dry and massive in her mouth and hurt her throat when she swallowed.

She had been saving her call to Naz till last because it was comforting to hold on to the idea that then, finally, she could be open and, maybe, even let some of the tears out. She felt instinctively that Naz would be able to hear how upset and frightened she was and know the right words to say to help her feel less wretched about herself.

By midnight, she told herself that it was 'for the best' that Naz hadn't answered her call. She wasn't sure what she would have said to her anyway. If she could have dared to risk being honest, it would have just made her sound vulnerable, and neurotic, and needy again. And surely she had done too much of that already, with the lift episode followed so rapidly by her cold feet in the hotel room and her meltdown at the flat on Sunday? The last thing Naz - or anyone else, for that matter - would want to be lumbered with, was a 'high maintenance' girlfriend.

She told herself it was all academic anyway. She hadn't got back to Naz in time and, bearing in mind all of the above, she'd probably given up on her.

There didn't seem to be anything left but to go to bed. And when she got there, she knew she was going to be haunted by guilt and the images she couldn't seem to shake, of Lydia Dryer where she'd left her in bed, last Monday and what that scene must have been like when her landlady finally found her six hot summer days later.

'Precious Nazzaro... Outside!... *NOW!*' Tracey was fuming, and who could blame her? Naz put the key back on its hook and slunk outside. She'd spent the night in the van, and despite the promise of a warm morning, she was shivering.

'Where the *FUCK* have you been?'

'I'm sorry!' She looked it too, standing there, hunched and wretched and smelling like... well, Tracey didn't want to dwell too much on quite what Naz smelt of.

'You're a sorry piece of shit, is what you are! And you still haven't answered me....'

'I went into Leeds.'

'For *ten* hours...? It's ten minutes down the road!'

Naz wrapped her arms around herself. Her teeth were chattering.

'I got drunk,' she said. 'And I daren't drive back, so I slept in the van.'

In fact, she hadn't slept at all, but had eventually climbed into the back of the van; curling up with her hands over her head and staring wretchedly into the darkness until dawn came and she could go to McDonalds for a coffee. She couldn't say any of that to Tracey. She felt too ashamed.

'I thought you'd driven to London,' said Tracey, softening somewhat at the relief of how much worse it could have been.

Naz shook her head. 'No,' she said, her eyes filling with tears. 'That's all over now.'

'God, love, what on *earth* were you thinking of?'

'I dunno. I guess I just wasn't thinking at all.'

'Well, I've really had to put my arse on the line for you with this caper. Had to bribe Jason in security with a catering pack of tea bags and twelve assorted tubs of ice cream... God, he drives a hard bargain does *that* one... I treated his first suggestion of a blow job with the contempt it deserved.'

Tears were streaming down Naz's face now... for the shame of last night... causing trouble for Tracey.... for losing Kate... and for just not having anyone to go home to when she felt bruised and battered by life and needed a bit of TLC.

Tracey shook her head. 'You gotta get a grip Naz,' she said. 'So, you got disappointed in love. Welcome to the human race. Go get yourself showered and changed. Are you fit to work? How hung over are you?'

'I feel pretty rough. But it serves me right. I'll get cleaned up and back on duty before anyone can even miss me.'

'Okay. And if this ever happens again... mate or not... you're out.... Do you hear me?'

'Yes.' Naz nodded glumly and slunk off in the direction of the staff quarters.

Tracey felt seriously worried for her as she watched her go.

'Any news on the Jarald Street case?' Peter Laclan looked up from his computer as Jamila walked past.

'God,' he thought, *'I love that woman.'* He couldn't help himself and he knew it was futile and hoped she would never know and pity him, wrapped up as she was in her apparently perfect life with her highly successful husband and beautiful house in Muswell Hill.

She frowned, realising that she'd farmed it out and hadn't pulled it back yet. They were both busy, and, to be honest, the probable suicide of yet another abused and unhappy woman wasn't high on her priority list.... even with the intriguing Kate Ferrings connection.

'I'll check on progress,' she said. 'See you back here in a couple of hours. I'll bring us cappuccinos and blueberry muffins from Nico's.'

'D'you know, there are more than four hundred calories in one of these.' She sat down next to Laclan on the dot of 3pm. She was slightly flushed, as if she'd just run up the stairs to get there on time. He thought she looked adorable. 'Well, you don't need to worry about your figure,' he said, then found himself blushing. 'I mean, not like me,' he pretended to pinch the flab around his midriff, but she thought he was in pretty good shape for an older guy, and wished he wouldn't keep putting himself down like that.

'Okay,' she said. 'First bit of bad news – Our Jane Doe wasn't actually called Lydia Dryer. It's not a particularly common name, especially in the right age group. But they're all very much alive and kicking.'

Laclan sighed and took a long swig of the coffee. 'I love this stuff!' he said appreciatively. 'It nearly blasts your head off!' He liked his coffee strong. It helped him get through the crazy shifts he had to do. He forced himself to concentrate back on the case in hand. 'I guess it makes sense that she would have been using a false name. It would fit with her being on the run from a violent partner. Maybe the refuge will have information that might help us join up the dots?'

'Yeah... I'll give them a ring, though 'Lydia' never actually stayed there. She used their support services for benefits advice, info about rooms to rent, and of course, to access the counselling with Kate. There's another interesting twist too.... The tox report just through says she was pretty much pumped full of diazepam... And there were also traces in the cup beside the bed, which is smothered in Kate Ferrings' fingerprints, There's no record of any drugs packaging at the scene, which would fit with the diazepam being brought in by someone planning to kill Lydia. And the actual cause of death was asphyxiation from the carrier bag over her head, which has three clear sets of finger prints and quite a few smudgy ones..... One of the clear sets is from the deceased, one unidentified, though it was the kind of cheap carrier they have in small shops and takeaways, so they're probably from there... and... I hate to say this... the other set belongs to Kate.'

Laclan groaned. 'The CI's gonna hate this. She's his golden girl.'

'I know.' Jamila took a sip of her coffee. 'And then there's the mystery of our anonymous tip-off. Who would do that? And why?'

'It could be genuine... Somebody just trying to help without getting involved.'

'Maybe.... Or it could be somebody with a grudge against Kate... after all, she's had a pretty meteoric rise to fame. People don't always like that.'

'True... Though she doesn't deny that she was there, so the report *is* accurate.'

'Mm... I don't know. I don't buy it. It's all a bit too messy for my liking.'

'What's *your* instinct about it then?' He trusted Jamila's instincts, just as he trusted everything else about her.

She shook her head. 'I don't know. We'll struggle to make suicide stick without a note or a bottle for the tablets. I'm wondering if Kate is keeping something from us. Like maybe she gave 'Lydia' some diazepam to help her calm down and it all went horribly wrong. I think we need to keep digging. I've got Jules Mullen trawling the Missing Person lists. She's like a dog with a bone when she gets going. If it's murder, the husband's got to be our most likely suspect, but without an ID for the deceased we're not going to find *him* very easily. I don't buy Kate Ferrings as a cold-blooded killer, even if she *is* the only suspect we've got at the moment. I reckon she's the kind of person who wouldn't even walk on the grass if there was a notice telling her not to. At a stretch, there's potentially a motive there, if she knew this woman was thinking of lodging a complaint. But it'd have to be something pretty damning to drug someone, hold a plastic bag over their head and leave them to rot for six days....'

'Sexual impropriety?' Laclan tilted his head slightly as he said it. 'That'd send the meteoric rise into an almighty crash and burn.'

Jamila laughed. 'Yeah... but Kathryn Ferrings?.. Can you imagine it?... Seriously...?'

'Well, I wouldn't kick her out of bed.'

'*Really?* I don't see it myself. She seems pretty buttoned up to me.'

'Precisely!' said Laclan. 'They're always the worst.'

Kate looked shocked to see them on her doorstep again. 'I'm sorry,' she said. 'I'm with a client.'

'That's okay, we can wait. Fifty minutes max, that's right, isn't it.'

'Not for a trauma debrief. But actually, we're almost done. Please, help yourselves to hot drinks if you like. I won't be long.'

They sat again, side by side on the sofa.

'Wonder if I'd find diazepam in the bathroom cabinet if I went to the toilet,' said Laclan.

'Wouldn't mean she administered it,' said Jamila quietly.

He looked around the room as they waited, remembering it from Monday. It was neat and tastefully decorated. Nice relaxing colours. Magnolia walls. Laclan was a big fan of magnolia. He liked the sage green of the carpet too. It felt calm.... which is more than anyone could say about its owner. There was no sign of any significant other, and everything looked about the same age. He reckoned Kate had probably bought it all when she moved into the flat, alone, maybe a couple of years ago.

'I like the picture,' he said. 'I went to the Whistler exhibition in Dulwich last year. It was good.'

Jamila smiled. It was amazing how much they had in common.

'I wish I'd known you were going, I would have loved to have come with you. Sayed has absolutely no interest in such things and it's no fun going alone.'

Laclan had lost track of how many times he'd done just that. And she was right, it *was* no fun.

'That would have been nice,' he said. In fact, on this occasion, he'd taken a woman he'd met on an internet dating site. It turned out that *she* had absolutely no interest in such things either.

Faintly, they heard Kate's voice in the hallway. 'I'm sorry again about the interruption Matthew... See you next week, same time.'

The door clicked shut.

Kate looked ashen as she came in. Jamila guessed that she hadn't been sleeping well, and wondered how she had managed to concentrate on her client, knowing that they were in the flat, waiting for her.

She sat in the armchair under the Whistler print.

'Is there any news?' she asked. 'About Lydia, I mean.'

'Well, she's not called Lydia Dryer for one,' said Laclan.

'No. I did wonder about that.... when she was so frightened of her husband finding her.'

'We were wondering if you could remember anything that might help us identify her... You know, maybe any details she gave you... husband's name... any kids.... brothers, sisters, any places she mentioned... There was no mention of any of that in the notes.'

'No, I don't put anything in there that could identify the client.'

The irony of this was not lost on any of them.

'Okay, let me think....' she closed her eyes, and Jamila could see her thinking back over her sessions with

"Lydia"..... She wondered about Laclan's comment about not kicking her out of bed, realising that she had felt a slight tremor of jealousy when he said that. She hastily shoved the thought out of her mind. Sayed was a good man, even if he had been late for the Eid celebrations this year and spent most of his spare time ignoring her and watching sport on Sky TV.

'She never named her husband,' said Kate. She had the slightly distant look of a medium at a séance. Jamila was aware that, like Peter and herself, she must have so many people in her head. She knew how easily they could all blur into each other. 'She didn't have any kids. She said she'd wanted to but he didn't. He had to keep her all to himself. She mentioned a mother and a sister, but she hadn't been able to tell them she was leaving her husband because they would have been on his side.... I'm sorry, I'm not being very helpful, am I? Have you spoken to the refuge, they might have more specific details.'

Jamila shook her head. They'd been keen to help when she phoned, but, like Kate, they just didn't seem to have the information. 'No,' she said. 'It would appear that she was very cagey with them too.'

Peter stepped in. 'There was a carrier bag at the scene. Blue and white stripes. Does it ring any bells with you?'

Kate nodded, pleased to have something she could help with. 'Yes, she'd brought some poetry the week before and left it here for me to read. It was in a carrier bag. I gave it back to her the day she...' she tailed off.

'The day she...?

'The day she died.' She swallowed.

'Was she on any medication?'

'Citalopram.... for her depression.'

'Nothing else?'

'Not that I know of? What does her doctor say? The GP details were in my notes... Oh, no, that's silly of me isn't it? If she gave a false name.... Though maybe it's worth seeing if she fits the description of anyone on his list....' She looked hopeful.

Laclan shook his head. 'We've already tried it.'

'Oh...' said Kate. 'I guess she made that up too then.... well, as far as I know, it was just Citalopram.'

'Is there anything else?' asked Laclan. 'Anything at all that might help us?'

Kate closed her eyes again, shook her head slowly as she ran back through the sessions. 'No,' she said. 'I got the feeling she didn't want to give too much away. She was frightened.... frightened that her husband would come after her. I never really felt that she entirely trusted me. And who could blame her?'

Laclan and Shah looked at each other. Jamila nodded as they both stood up.

'Okay. Thank you Ms Ferrings... I know you're busy.... And you've been very helpful. We may be able to find out more through "Lydia's" landlady.'

Kate walked behind them to the door. Her head was aching and her next client was due in fifteen minutes. She couldn't wait for them to be gone.

Laclan turned round on the doorstep, and she took a step back involuntarily.

'And you still can't think why she might have wanted to file a complaint?' he asked.

She felt sick.... fought against the tears threatening to rise into her eyes as she shook her head.

'I torture myself constantly with that question,' she said. 'And truly, I have absolutely no idea.'

Kate's website should have been the perfect antidote for Naz's lovesickness.

Clearly designed by some slick internet consultant - the corporate styling, sound-bite wording, shameless bragging about qualifications, experience and effectiveness – not to mention the fees, which made Naz's eyes widen in amazement – should all have served to remind her of the less than attractive aspects of Kate's personality. And they did.

But there was also a photograph, professionally taken and slightly soft focus, and a 'Personal Statement' that almost ripped Naz's heart out of her chest with its disarming sweetness, and she found her thoughts rushing to where they wanted to be, with Kate, lying in her arms, hearing the soft thud of her heart and feeling a sense of peace that she'd never really experienced in her life before.

So she hovered around the website like a ghost, tied by guilt and longing, disconnected by time and space and the sick, juddering memory of where Jess's hands had been. And she found herself frozen... unable to either return or move on.

The desk sergeant looked like he'd eaten too many bacon butties in his thirty year police career. He was bored and jaded and counting the days to retirement when he intended to retreat to a nice little place by the sea at Eastbourne. Even so, he had a nose for a genuine case and he smelt that now. He ambled down the ranks of desks until he got to DC Jules Mullen.

'Jules,' he said, as she looked up at him through her thick glasses. 'I reckon I've just found your MISPER.'

Mike Ryder didn't actually look like a thug.

'She was the love of my life,' he wept, trying to un-ball the paper tissues in his hand so that he could blow his nose on them again. Jamila gently nudged a box of fresh tissues towards him. It always felt strange to her to see a man crying. Her father had never cried, not even when her mother died. And Sayed? Well, Sayed was made of sterner stuff too. Mike pulled a handful of tissues out of the box, accidentally shredding a few in the process and leaving a trail of Kleenex crumbs across the desk. 'I knew from the very first moment I saw her,' he continued, through great, heaving sobs that lifted his shoulders and dragged at his chest. 'She was the only woman for me.'

Peter Laclan felt sorry for him, sitting there, pitiful and washed up and alone with his grief. He wondered if Ryder would ever be able to expunge this day from his memory.

'How was it that you were living apart?' he asked quietly.

Ryder's jaw trembled as he worked to form words. He gave up the struggle. 'I'm sorry,' he gasped, sinking into sobs again.

They waited.

'She told me she didn't love me anymore,' he said finally. 'I don't know why. I worked so hard to get her everything she wanted.... Working away from home for weeks on end.... It's not an easy life.'

'So... what changed?'

'I don't know. It was her. She was always wild. A bit cruel. She liked to hurt me. It was just how she was. It kept me on my toes. I think... I don't know. And she'd play around a bit. That was always part of the deal. We had rules about that. So long as she told me, you know. But then there was this guy. And she didn't tell me. I found stuff... photos... texts.'

'So you hit her.... I mean, when you found that?'

Ryder looked horrified. 'God, no. I'd never hit her... *never...* not once. She used to batter me. It turned us both on. But I'd never hit a woman. I'm not like that.'

Jamila leaned forward. She didn't believe him. 'Mr Ryder, these photographs.... do you still have copies of them?'

'No... they were on her computer... and on her phone.'

'Could you describe them for us?'

'They were pictures of her and him. Private pictures. You know.'

'Together?'

'No.'

'Okay.... ' She pictured the kind of thing. She'd seen them so many times. In so many shapes and sizes. Sometimes she felt wistful for the days when such things still shocked her.

He gulped from the plastic cup of vile coffee they had set in front of him and made a strange half strangled kind of sniffling sound.

'I can see how that must have upset you. You'd been working hard trying to provide for her. And you had your agreement. And she'd been doing that behind your back. What did you do with them when you found them?'

'I smashed them.'

'The phone?'

'Yes.'

'And the computer?'

'Yes.'

'Was she frightened when you did that?'

'No - Rach wasn't frightened of anything or anybody. She just laughed in my face. Told me I was pathetic. That she'd only have to replace them now and I'd have to pay for them.'

'I can see how that could have made you angry.'

He shook his head. 'No,' he said. 'That "pathetic" thing. It always turned me on. We had the best sex we'd had in years.'

'But then she left you.'

'Yes.' He sniffled again, defeated, into a fresh tissue, dropping the others onto the table.

Jamila wondered, distantly, if she would be the one who had to clean them up.

'And so, you didn't try to stop her leaving?' she asked. She was surprised at the thought nagging within her that, yes, this man *was* pathetic. She closed her eyes and took a deep breath. Maybe this was what Kate Ferrings would call countertransference. Whatever it was, it wasn't helpful. She tried to force the thought out of her mind.

'No... how could I? She always did exactly what she wanted. I figured if I just sat it out, bided my time, waited for her to get disillusioned with this new guy... Then she might realise what she'd lost, and come back to me.'

'What *do* you think she'd lost?' Jamila hadn't expected the harshness in her voice until the words were out.

She felt Laclan flinch slightly beside her.

But Mike Ryder didn't seem to mind the question. 'Lovely house... plenty of money... nice holidays... And somebody who loves you, no matter what,' he said gently. 'Me and her against the world. That's how it always was.'

Laclan stepped in.

'So what made you report her missing now?' he asked.

'She stopped texting. At first I thought it was just one of her games, and I was working in Glasgow so there wasn't much I could do. But as soon as I got back home, I went round there... and her landlady told me what had happened. She called her Lydia, but I knew it was Rach.... Lydia was her second name, you see. God knows what tales she'd been telling the old bird... She looked so frightened of me... tried to shut the door in my face... threatened to call you lot if I didn't go. So I came straight here, and, well... you know the rest.'

Laclan barely missed a beat. 'So you're saying she was still in contact with you?'

'Yeah... of course. She was in touch all the time. Text and phone. The new boyfriend wasn't all he was cracked up to be. Right waste of space, in fact. Sat on his arse all day, playing with his-self and smoking pot. And that old biddy at the Jarald Street place. Rach never *could* stand wrinklies. She was driving her nuts, twittering on all the time. She wanted to come home. She used to text three or four times a day. Mainly telling me how I'd have to shape up if she came back. But that was okay. I could do that. And then the texts just stopped, last Monday.'

'Have you saved any of them?' asked Laclan.

'Yeah. All of 'em.' He pulled a Samsung Galaxy out of his pocket and shoved it across the desk in Peter's direction. 'See for yourself. Keep it if it helps. I never phone anybody but Rach.'

'Thank you sir. We'll check through those.... And could I just clarify with you how long you've known where your wife was living?'

'Ever since she left home. She gave me the address before she moved in. Why wouldn't she?' His mouth started contorting again and Jamila thought there would be more tears, but he managed to control himself. 'I want you to get the bastard who did this,' he said, shifting suddenly into anger.

'Are you aware of anyone who might have had a grudge against your wife?... How about her boyfriend... if he knew she was thinking of returning home...?'

'Jed Watkins, 11c Cramley Heights,' he said, helpfully. Jamila rapidly scribbled it down.

'How did you find out his name and address?'

'Followed him.'

'From Jarald Street?'

'Yeah... about six weeks ago.'

'So, you were watching your wife's movements?'

'Sometimes. Wouldn't you? If it were your husband, having an affair?'

She didn't answer. 'Anyone else who might have had a grudge against Rachel?'

He laughed bitterly. 'More like who *didn't*,' he said. 'I told you, she was a right bitch.... pissed everybody off eventually.'

'Okay... there's no easy way to ask this...' Peter leaned forward and Jamila sat back, as if affording them privacy – man to man. 'But we need to rule it out as a possibility. Your wife was obviously very... open-minded... sexually... I mean.... Is there any way this could have been a sex-game gone wrong?'

'No way,' he shook his head vehemently. 'She tried it once. Scared the shit out of her. There's no way she'd ever do that again.'

'And you don't think it could have been suicide?'

'No chance. She wasn't the suicide type – and even if she *had* been, she wouldn't have done it like that. It'd have just been pills and a bottle of vodka for Rach. We talked about it. Like if either of us ever got terminally ill. You know the kind of thing.'

'Yes,' said Laclan, who was prone to dwelling on those kinds of thoughts from time to time. 'I do.' He leaned back, making the way clear for Jamila.

'Would it be possible for us to have a recent photograph of your wife?' she asked gently, not wanting to set him off crying again.

He nodded. 'There's loads on my phone. You can print 'em off if you like.'

'Okay, thank you. I'll get a consent form for you before you leave..... Did you know your wife was seeing a therapist?'

He gave a short, bitter half-cough of laughter. 'No way! Rach thought all that stuff was a right old con. One of Rachel's victims at school became a therapist. Rach used to laugh her head off about it.'

Jamila felt the sharp jolt of adrenalin she always associated with a breakthrough. 'What do you mean by "victim"?' she asked quietly.

'Oh, bullying.... you know what girls are like. They're worse than lads if you ask me. All that emotional torture they go in for. She made this kid's life a misery.'

'Can you remember her name?'

Mike Ryder paused, thinking, then shook his head. 'God... what *was* it? I quite liked her. But Rach had a right downer on her for some reason.'

'Did she have a nickname... this girl?' Distantly Jamila remembered the bullies at her own school. There was almost always a nickname, something that could be hurled across the playground like a missile.

He closed his eyes.... 'Shit... what did they call her..? I can picture her.... scrawny little thing... Her parents were getting on a bit when they had her and she always looked really old-fashioned..... They were in some bonkers religious group and they wouldn't let her wear tights or make-up or any of that stuff.... But I always thought she was a nice kid. Her and Rach seemed like they were getting to be good friends at one point, but it didn't last. Rach'll have done something to spoil it. She always did. God, what was that nickname? I remember thinking at the time, it described her quite well... Fffff....fff...' for a moment, he sounded like a kid learning to read....

Jamila held her breath.

'Ferret!' he said, triumphantly.

'Ferret?.... Kate Ferrings?'

'Yeah... that's right. Little Katie Ferrings.... how did you know that?' He looked suspicious suddenly.

'Oh, she just does some work for the Met. She's done quite well for herself.'

'Ah... well, good for *her*. I always thought she would.' Then he crumpled. 'Mebbe now she's a psychologist, she could help you find out who killed my Rach.'

Laclan got the cappuccinos this time. He'd noticed that Jamila looked weary and he wanted to take care of her, but she'd turned down his offer of cake. She always lost her appetite when she was tired. It worried him.

'This is turning out to be a right old can o'worms!' he said, struggling with the packaging on his own slice of flapjack.

She took it from him and opened it, which is what he'd been angling for all along. 'There's a knack,' she said.

'Thanks. D'you want a bit?'

'Just a corner then.'

'Okay... to recap.... We'll need to double-check with the dental records, but if Mike Ryder's to be believed, Lydia Dryer is actually Rachel Lydia Ryder... *not* a battered wife... and *not* hiding from her husband. She has a list of enemies as long as your arm. And she was *at school* with Kate Ferrings.... A fact that, for reasons not yet clear, Kate has chosen to keep from us.... thereby making this whole investigation considerably harder than it ever needed to be.'

'Yeah... It's not looking good for our Golden Girl, is it?'

'Nope....' Laclan took a swig of his coffee. 'What do you reckon?'

Jamila sighed. 'Let's leave Kate to stew for a bit. I'd like to have a word with the boyfriend anyway.... And another chat with Mrs Morgan, the landlady... Let's see if she remembers Rachel having any visitors.'

"The boyfriend" was pretty much as Mike Ryder had described. Twenty four years old, and with a string of minor convictions for crimes that didn't take much effort – handling stolen goods, non-payment of fines, no tax, MOT, or insurance on his car, and, when they looked more deeply, no driving licence either.

Jamila could see what someone like Rachel might have found attractive about him, initially, at least. He was handsome in a 'bad boy' kind of way. He also looked like a man who would enjoy playing with himself for the camera, provided he didn't have to venture too far from his sofa to do it. But he must have become a disappointment very quickly for any woman who didn't want to be at the bottom of Jed's already very low-priority list of things to do.

'Is it about the car again?' he asked, when he opened the door and saw their ID cards.

'Not this time mate. It's about the girlfriend.'

Behind him, the flat reeked of weed. The television set (almost certainly massive, flat screen and 'off the back of a lorry') was booming its way through the daytime TV adverts which were vying with drum and bass from the flat next door. He didn't invite them in. 'Which one?' He scratched his chest slowly through his black T-shirt, which appeared to have a dribble of egg down the front.

'Lydia Dryer?'

He looked blank.

'You might know her as Rachel Ryder.'

'Nah...'

Jamila showed him the photograph they'd chosen of Rachel, looking beautiful on a beach in Sardinia, her blonde hair tumbling over her shoulders as she smiled for the camera.

'Oh, yeah.' Jed kept scratching. Jamila figured, if they searched his flat, that they'd find cocaine as well as cannabis... 'Rach,' he said. 'What's she done?'

'She's got herself killed.'

'Oh, right,' he shrugged. 'Well, that's nothing to do with me.'

His story matched perfectly with Mike's. He'd met "Rach" in a bar. He knew she was married. He liked them that way. No ties. They'd gone in for some heavy duty on-line and phone sex. Then she'd got "way too intense"; left her husband; moved into the flat on Jarald Street; become 'high maintenance'.

'So you decided to get rid of her?' asked Peter.

'Yeah... but not like you're meaning.... Just the usual.... Not answering me phone, not getting back to her texts, ignoring her voice mails. You know the sort of thing. They get the message eventually.'

'And "Rach" had *she* got the message.'

'Yeah, she was going back to hubby. Best thing for her. Nice carry-on she had there. Should never have left.'

'Did you ever visit her at her place in Jarald Street?'

He was still scratching. Jamila felt like slapping his hand away. He smirked as he saw her looking. 'Well, you know. When it's laid out on a plate for you...'

Peter felt like slapping him too, though not particularly for the scratching. He took out his notebook instead. 'Some dates and times would be good,' he said. 'For the purposes of elimination, you understand.'

Jarald Street was a typical North London residential road. It had large Victorian houses that were now almost all converted into flats or bedsits or house-shares. On the right hand side there was a huddle of small shops – a hairdresser, catering mainly to the over seventies, a florist with a few sad pots of heather outside, and a fish and chip shop, founded in 1951 and passed down through generation after generation of the aptly named Spratt family. Between the florist and the chippy, and almost directly opposite Number Five, was the small Pay and Display car park where the anonymous informant had claimed... and she, herself, had later confirmed... that Kate had parked her car on the day she brought her client home.

Mrs Morgan was embarrassed at being caught in her pink chenille housecoat and slippers, but she was anxious after Mike's visit, ('I don't know how that dreadful man had the nerve to turn up here?') and keen to invite them in and treat them as guests with 'proper' tea and biscuits.

The cups were china, with a pretty blue floral pattern, and the biscuits (arrowroot, and chocolate fingers) had a matching plate.

Jamila felt grateful for the tea. She was sitting rather too close to Peter on a very upright, two-seater Ercol settee, facing a fireplace with a large dried flower arrangement and a carved oak mantelpiece with a mirror above it. There were framed photographs on the mantelpiece. She guessed that the one on the right, a slightly faded professional photograph of a smiling young woman in University Graduation robes, was probably the daughter in Southsea. She wondered about its companion on the left - a handsome young man in army dress uniform.

'My son, Andrew,' said the old lady, seeing her looking. 'He was killed in action during the Gulf War...'

'I'm so sorry.'

'Thank you. He was a hero, though I'm not sure that helps very much really. And that, of course, is my daughter Isobel.'

'I thought it must be. You must miss them both... in very different ways of course.' God, was that really inept?

If it was, the old lady either didn't notice, or didn't mind.

'Yes. I wish Izzie lived closer. I've missed seeing the grandchildren growing up... and now, the great grandchildren too. But, I don't blame her for moving away. Her father was... difficult... Please...' she urged, changing the subject abruptly. 'Do have another biscuit. Neither of you look like you need to be on diets... Unlike me, I'm afraid. It's the arthritis. I can't exercise as much as I would like, and then, of course, I pile weight on, which makes the arthritis worse, and so it goes, in ever decreasing circles!'

Laclan nodded sympathetically and, as always, couldn't resist a second chocolate finger.

Jamila declined. 'We're sorry to disturb you again, Mrs Morgan,' she began as he munched.

'Nancy, please.'

'Nancy... thank you. As I say, we're very sorry to disturb you again, but we're still trying to piece together what happened to your tenant...'

'Ah, poor Lydia.'

'Yes...'

The elderly lady's lip trembled. She fumbled in the pocket of her house-coat for a handkerchief – proper linen, with an ornate NM embroidered in the corner.

'...And we wondered if she may have said anything at all to you that could help us?'

The old lady shook her head. 'I doubt it. Lydia never really confided in me... not like Jackie, my last tenant... *she* was more like a friend than a lodger. She still comes to visit me sometimes you know, even though she has her own flat now. I think she feels sorry for me rattling around in this big old house on my own. She's terribly upset about all this I'm afraid.'

'Yes, she told me how helpful you were to her when she had to leave her husband a couple of years ago. She said that was why she recommended you to Lydia. She thought it would be a nice friendly place for her to stay while she was getting back on her feet.'

'Yes, Jackie's a lovely young woman. Very open-hearted.... Lydia was very different.'

Jamila remembered Mike Ryder's description of his wife. 'So Lydia wasn't friendly?'

Nancy frowned, weighing up the word. 'She wasn't *un*-friendly,' she said. 'In fact, she could be quite charming.

But she kept herself to herself. I imagine it was because she was frightened and upset.'

'Yes – I guess so.... Did you take up any references for her before she moved in here?'

'Oh goodness, no! It never occurred to me. She was in such a difficult situation. Do you think I should have done?'

'Well, it might be safer, in future.'

Mrs Morgan shook her head. 'I couldn't have anyone else,' she said. 'Not after this.' She dabbed at her eyes with the handkerchief. 'Hay fever,' she said, unconvincingly.

Jamila knew that Victim Support must have been in touch. But she doubted that this sad and highly self-sufficient old lady would have taken up their offer of help. She wished that she would. It was all clearly still preying on her mind.

Peter had finished his biscuit. 'Did Lydia have many visitors?' he asked, wiping crumbs from his mouth before draining his teacup.

Mrs Morgan shook her head again, but it was the kind of shake that suggested that she was thinking. 'She went out a lot, and always looked very well turned out when she did. Though perhaps she wasn't always wisely dressed if she was hoping to avoid male attention. She had one friend who came round sometimes. A rather masculine looking woman, a little bit rude. Never really acknowledged me when I said "Hello" to her in the hallway.'

They both looked up hopefully. 'Did she mention a name?'

'Not that I remember.'

'Anything else that might help us trace her? Anything distinctive about her?'

'She had short, straight, dark hair... possibly dyed. She looked about the same age as Lydia, thirtyish. Medium height, though she wore heels, so it's hard to know. She was usually dressed quite professionally in dark trouser suits.'

'Did she have a car?'

'I didn't notice.'

'Okay. Thank you. Was there anyone else?'

'There was a young man who came to fix her computer.... I didn't like the look of him at all... A bit of a handsome devil, but very shifty, if you ask me... early twenties probably.... *He* came a couple of times. I wouldn't have let him anywhere near *my* computer, I can tell you. He looked like he'd be accessing your personal data the minute your back was turned.'

'You have a computer?' asked Peter, impressed.

'Of course I have a computer. However else would I keep in touch with the grandchildren?'

'Anyone else?'

'Only the counsellor.'

'The counsellor?.... are you sure?'

'Yes. I remember specifically because I was worried when I heard the door go at that time of night. I know how frightened Lydia was of her husband, you see.... so I actually went upstairs to make sure everything was alright.'

Jamila saw the shudder, as a later image of going up those stairs flashed, unbidden into the old lady's mind.

'What happened?' she asked, hoping to distract her from the horror of that.

'Lydia came to her door.... I can remember her exact words. Isn't that strange? Maybe it's because she didn't talk to me very often... "Please don't worry Mrs Morgan" she said... She never could get into the habit of calling me Nancy... "It's just my counsellor. I've been having a difficult evening."..... I thought that was very kind of the lady, don't you? I think she was seeing Lydia for nothing too. Jackie had arranged it for her through the refuge.'

'Yes,' said Peter hastily. 'Very kind... Did you see what the counsellor looked like?'

'No, Lydia only opened the door slightly. I imagined that was because of confidentiality or some such. Counsellors have quite strict rules, don't they?'

Not generally to protect the identity of the *counsellor* though, thought Peter. Did you notice a car outside?'

'No, but all the residents have parking permits, so almost everyone else uses the Pay and Display.'

Peter nodded. 'Did this just happen once?' he asked. 'The counsellor coming round, I mean?'

'No. But the next two times Lydia popped a note under my door so that I wouldn't be worried. She *was* very thoughtful like that.'

'Bloody hell!' said Peter as they closed Mrs Morgan's small wrought iron gate and stepped out onto the tree-lined pavement.

'It wasn't necessarily Kate,' said Jamila. 'After all, Rachel claimed that Jed was "fixing her computer".'

'Yeah... well, I've never heard it called that before!'

They both laughed, weakly.

'Okay, well, thankfully, our Mrs Morgan's sharp as a tack. Let's get Jules onto the CCTV footage at the Pay and Display and see if there's any sign of our mystery midnight counsellor.'

Naz was trying to put a brave face on things. 'What's the definition of "Psychological Change" for Kate Ferrings?' she asked as she ambled into the lobby and saw Saskia and Tracey giggling conspiratorially over the reception desk.

'Dunno,' said Tracey. 'What *is* the definition of "Psychological Change" for Kate Ferrings?'

'Nowt out of eighty quid an hour!' said Naz, triumphantly. 'Boom boom!!!'

They both laughed.

And Naz laughed too, at her own joke, though there was a part of her that felt a bit bad about it, if she was honest. She told herself it was therapeutic.

'Seriously though,' she said. 'Eighty quid an hour... how extortionate is *that*?... Guess I'm lucky she didn't charge *me* for her services, eh?... I'd have had to take all me worldly goods to Cash Convertor's to pay for her!'

And they all laughed again, though Tracey couldn't help but worry that Naz might be spending all her spare time mooning around Kate's website when she ought to be picking herself up and moving on.

Kate knew what they wanted the moment she saw their faces.

'May we come in?' asked Peter Laclan, keen not to cause a scene on the doorstep.

Kate let them into the hallway. She didn't take them any further. She didn't want them in her sitting room again, though she knew they would go in there - that they could just go wherever they liked now and she would have no right to stop them.

'We have a warrant to search these premises.'

She nodded. 'Okay. You'd better do it then.... Can I just explain what's going on to this gentleman?' She had spotted her next client, coming up the front path, looking bewildered at the sight of Laclan and Shah. Kate stepped outside and the two spoke for several minutes. DC Mullen watched from the car, where she was sitting with a Scenes of Crime Officer. It was the first time Jules had seen Kate in person, though, of course, she knew her by repute and she recognised her from the grainy images she'd found on the CCTV footage, getting out of the black C1 she could see parked now on the street outside Kate's flat. She noticed that Kate touched the young man's arm reassuringly as he turned back towards the road. She thought she looked kind, which didn't fit at all with what she may have done at the flat on Jarald Street. But then, Jules had soon learnt when she joined the Met, that appearances could be very deceptive indeed.

Jamila led Kate into the kitchen, where she indicated for her to sit down at the table.

Kate didn't offer any drinks this time. She sat and Jamila sat beside her.

'What are you looking for?' asked Kate.

'Evidence relating to our investigation.'

'Right!'

'I realise this must all be deeply distressing for you.'

'*Do* you?'

Jamila bridled. 'At least we now know who "Lydia Dryer" was' she said.

'Oh?' Kate sat up.

'Yes. Her husband reported her missing.'

'*Her husband?*'

'Yes, *we* thought that was odd too. But it turns out he was in touch with her all along.'

'You're kidding!'

'Her name is Rachel Lydia Ryder.'

Jamila looked closely into Kate's face and saw only utter blankness there. 'Or you might know her better by her maiden name... Rachel Stiles.'

Jamila saw Kate go into shock. It didn't look like the shock of someone who thought they'd got away with something and hadn't. But there was something... something she couldn't quite place... something that looked suspiciously like guilt... 'No,' Kate shook her head. 'It wasn't Rachel. Truly it wasn't. I would have recognised her.'

In a brief moment of insanity though, she couldn't feel so sure. Maybe Rachel had disguised herself deliberately? That was the kind of thing she would do, wasn't it? Set out to trick her... fool her .... *test* her again and finally destroy her? Could somebody *do* that? Someone you'd seen day in day out for seven years? Someone whose every inch... every expression, every vocal nuance was scorched into your memory? Someone who'd done what Rachel did that night, all those years ago? Kate looked wildly around the familiar space of her kitchen trying to find something to fix her attention on.... some way of anchoring the world that was spinning dangerously out of control.

'It isn't too late to tell us the truth,' said Jamila gently.

Kate felt tears stinging at the back of her eyes. 'I *have* told you the truth,' she said. 'It wasn't Rachel. She looked a bit like Rachel. But she wasn't, I promise you.'

'Okay then. Maybe you'd like to tell me about her.'

'About Rachel?' Kate could hear the cold, clipped tone that always came into her voice when she was upset. It alienated people. She knew that. But now it had taken hold, she couldn't force it out. Or get the warmth back in.

'Yes. Tell me about Rachel,' said Jamila.

Kate didn't want to go back there. It was too painful. And the thought of Rachel being dead was painful too. Painful and unthinkable.

'I was at school with her. She was ... not a nice person.'

But I loved her, screamed a voice inside that wanted to tell the whole of the truth and couldn't. *I had a stupid, hopeless, adolescent crush on the prettiest girl in the school and she used it against me... Humiliated me... caused me to do things I hated myself for. And now she appears to be dead... and I feel devastated at the thought of her dying alone, rotting in that room for days, alone. What kind of a person am I to feel all this..? What kind of person am I really?*

'I had a bit of a crush on her, if I'm honest,' said Kate, trying to be as open as she could. 'But she was sadistic... cruel... She got her kicks out of hurting people.... Not just me.... lots of people. But, there's been some big mistake here. I haven't seen Rachel since I left school. I heard that she'd married her boyfriend... Mike. I remember now that his surname was Ryder. He was a couple of years older than us. Good looking. Drove a boy-racer car with go-fast stripes down the side. He was a really good footballer. At one point he was in the Under 21 squad for one of the big London clubs. I don't know whether that ever came to anything, but I think Rachel fancied being a footballer's wife. I doubt that she ever worked when she left school. I doubt whether that was *ever* part of the plan. But I'd struggle to imagine Mike hitting her. He was too much under her thumb... completely besotted. I went to University and then I did my therapy training. And our paths never crossed again. We weren't ever going to be 'Friends' on Facebook. But I know I would have recognised her instantly if she'd walked in here, even after twelve years.'

'How did she bully you?'

'Oh the usual stuff. You know how it goes. She was really cool and popular and I was a bit of a geek. I wanted to do well and make Mum and Dad proud of me. I don't know why I bothered. It never really worked.' She gave a little half laugh. It sounded... what was the word? Ironic, maybe? 'For some reason, Rachel and her gang seemed to single me out. Then when my friend Sue came along, they eased off me and turned on her.'

'Who were the gang?'

Kate chewed on her lip, remembering. 'Sally Ballantree and Julie Groves. They were like Crabbe and Goyle in the Harry Potter books. They usually meted out the "punishment" if people didn't comply with Rachel's requests. And actually, they were the ones who did the name calling and threatening, though it was always very clear that Rachel was the boss. One look from her and they'd fall into line.'

'Were they actually violent?'

'Sometimes...' For a moment, Jamila thought she was going to say more, but she didn't. 'Once they'd got people frightened enough they didn't need to be.'

'Do you know what happened to them?'

'Sally got pregnant. She's a single parent now, she's living in a high rise place in Tottenham.'

'How do you know?'

'My parents mentioned it. My mum was at school with her grandmother.'

'And Julie?'

'Julie's running a bar. I don't know what it's called.'

'It's okay, we can find out.' Jamila scribbled down the details in her notebook. Then she leaned forward, quietly... 'Kate, can you account for your movements between 11.30pm and 1am on Friday 6th, 13th and 20th June this year?'

Kate looked puzzled. 'I don't know. I would have been in bed, I guess. I work Saturday mornings, so I usually try to get to bed by about 10pm... Why?'

'Is there anyone who can verify that?'

'What, you mean, was I sleeping with anyone?' Kate felt herself starting to blush, embarrassed by her loneliness. 'No...' she thought of Naz, and felt her heart shudder at the loss. 'I don't have a partner.'

'Does anyone else have use of your car?'

'No,' Kate shook her head.

'Does anyone have a spare key to this flat... a friend maybe, neighbour... cleaner?'

'No.'

'Where do you keep your keys?'

'In a drawer - here in the kitchen.'

'Do you mind if I look?'

'No.' In a daze, Kate stood and opened the drawer. It was next to the fridge, under the microwave. It held a small First Aid Kit, a few rubber bands and spare light bulbs, a bunch of keys on a key ring and a selection of others in an open wooden desk-tidy.

Jamila stood beside her. 'Are they all there?'

'Yes... Look, what's all this about?'

Out of the corner of her eye, Jamila saw Peter Laclan in the doorway. He beckoned to her.

'Excuse me,' she said, quietly to Kate.

Kate watched as they spoke in low voices out in the hallway. Laclan's tone sounded flat and firm, Jamila's more animated. She shook her head as Laclan nodded, contradicting her. Then she hung back in the hall as Laclan came through into the kitchen. He had that look that police officers get sometimes, as if they're focusing on a point somewhere behind you.

What came next felt like it had been creeping towards Kate for years. She had no idea how to evade it anymore.

'Kate,' he said, gently. 'Could you explain why you are in possession of these items?'

He held up two evidence bags. One contained a mobile phone. The second had a bottle of diazepam.

Kate felt herself starting to shake. 'The diazepam's mine,' she said. 'I get quite anxious sometimes.'

'And your GP prescribes these?'

She could hear his surprise. Shame washed through her. A therapist who needed to resort to tranquillisers. She knew how bad that must look. She looked down at the floor.

'They're only for emergencies,' she said.

'And what about this?' He held up the bag with the phone.

'I've never seen it before in my life.'

'Are you sure Kate? Please take a good look.'

She lifted her head and eyed it warily, as if it might bite her. 'Yes, I'm sure,' she said.

'So can you explain how it might have ended up at the back of your wardrobe?'

'I've no idea.'

'Does anyone else have access to this flat?'

'No... I've just been through this with DS Shah.'

In the hallway, Jamila had been joined by the person who looked like he might be taking forensic samples. It felt chillingly unreal for Kate to see someone dressed like that in her home. He was holding another clear bag. It had an A4 manila envelope in it. He glanced over, covertly at Kate as he whispered something to DS Shah.

Laclan looked at Jamila, who lifted her hands in a gesture of surrender. He turned back to face Kate.

'Kathryn Ferrings...' he said. **'I am arresting you on suspicion of the murder of Rachel Lydia Ryder...'**

Over his shoulder, Kate saw Jamila look down at the floor. She willed her to look up, to catch her eye, to step in and do something, anything, to stop this happening.

'No,' said Kate. 'I'm telling you the truth. I was just explaining to DS Shah... Please believe me. It wasn't Rachel. She looked a bit like Rachel but it wasn't her. I would have recognised her....' She backed away, into the corner by the sink. Outside, through the window, she could hear the giddy sound of children playing in one of the neighbour's gardens. The tap was dripping. She needed to get it fixed.

'... You do not have to say anything... but it may harm your defence....'

'Please no... I'm claustrophobic... please don't lock me up....'

Jamila Shah looked up then, but not at Kate. At the end of the day, her loyalty was to her job. She knew that Peter was right. They had no choice but to do this, whatever, her 'gut' told her. And they could both see that Kate wasn't going to come quietly.

'... if you do not mention when questioned... something which you later rely on in court... Anything you do say may be taken down and given in evidence.'

Kate showed no sign of moving. She lashed out when Jamila stepped into the room and reached for her arm.

'I'm sorry, Kate, I really didn't want to have to do this.'

Kate closed her eyes against the inevitable.

Jamila could feel her shaking as she slid the cuffs onto her wrists.

Naz was drilling one of the guest room walls to re-hang a picture that had fallen down in the middle of the night. She had taken her shoes off and was standing, rather precariously, on the bed in her socks. Tracey, as usual, was directing operations.

'D'ya think they'll sue?' yelled Naz over the screaming of the Black and Decker.

'Dunno – they were talking about PTSD last I heard. Shame your ex isn't still here. She could have made herself useful. Whitlass offered them an extra night free, but they went a bit hysterical at that point.'

'Don't blame 'em. Bloody thing only just missed decapitating them....' Naz, pretended she hadn't flinched inside at the mention of Kate. 'Your phone's ringing, by the way!'

'What?'

'Your phone....'

'Oh, yeah. Is it okay if I answer it?' Saskia's name was flashing on the screen.

'Sure!' Naz braced herself against the wall. She had a horrible feeling she was up against a metal girder, which, presumably was why the picture hook had never been secure enough in the first place. Metal girders were a hazard of the sixties construction of the place and a constant source of frustration for Naz. The walls were full of them.

'Okay, back in a mo!' Tracey snatched the phone off the bed and clicked the green button to answer, backing out of the room and into the corridor where she could actually hear Saskia.

'Hi Sash!' she said, clicking the door shut to trap the worst of the noise inside the room.

'Big problem!' said the receptionist. 'Down! Now!'

Tracey sometimes felt like a dog being ordered about when Saskia was in full flow. There was something unresistable about the way she delivered orders though. She obeyed instantly, abandoning Naz to any Health and Safety violations she might be committing and pelting downstairs into the lobby.

'What's going on?' she asked breathlessly as she skidded to a halt by the desk.

'Big problem!' Saskia had one of the guests' discarded tabloid newspaper open on the desk in front of her. She turned it round to show her, jabbing at the page for emphasis.

'Oh fuck!' said the Hospitality Manager.

'Yes... fuck is right!!!!'

They both stared glumly at the sizeable headline halfway down page four.

'Trauma Specialist Quizzed Over Client Death'

'Was looking for horoscope,' said Saskia with a sigh. 'Found this.'

'What the hell are we gonna do?'

'Don't know!' Saskia glowered at the paper as if she could erase the offending headline by sheer force of will. 'Think we have to tell her,' she said eventually.

'Okay. But if she nicks that van again I'm *seriously* gonna have to kill her.'

As if on cue Naz came careering into the lobby. 'Just off to B&Q for some new drill bits' she mouthed. 'Bit of an accident with the last one!'

Tracey took a deep breath and smoothed out the paper. 'We just need to show you something first,' she said.

They watched Naz's hand creep up to her mouth as she read the article. 'Oh God,' she groaned when she'd finished. 'And I've been a total bitch about her.'

'You weren't to know.' Tentatively, Tracey put her hand on Naz's arm.

'I *should* have known. She's not the kind of person who just wouldn't get back without a good reason.'

'Well, the important thing is that you know now.' Tracey didn't really 'do' soothing, though she was trying her best and managing to keep her voice just on the right side of not irritated.

'I have to go to London.'

'No you bloody well do *not*! I don't know what's got into you since you met that woman. Just give her a bell for God's sake. It's not like she's been arrested or anything.'

'Okay,' Naz could see the sense in this. 'Is it okay if I try her now?'

'Yes, of course... Go back to your room if you want a bit of privacy. I'll cover for you here if Whitlass comes on the prowl.

They exchanged glances as Naz sloped off in the direction of the staff quarters. Then Tracey headed for the kitchens. 'I'm going to hide that bloody van key,' she said. 'And if she says anything more about going to B & Q tell her Whitlass has said we have to leave the room as it is until Health and Safety have had chance to look at it.'

To be fair to Naz, she tried very hard to reach Kate by phone. She rang from her room and dutifully left a voicemail 'after the beep'. Then about an hour later, she texted. Then she texted again. When there was still no reply, she sent an email through Kate's website.
Nothing.

By teatime, she was talking about going to London again and Saskia and Tracey were trying very hard to dissuade her.

'We need you here,' Tracey said bluntly.

'Is stupid!' This was Saskia.

'But...' Naz was starting to take on a pleading look.

They both glared at her.

Then, suddenly, Saskia said 'Ah!' with the air of someone who's just had a bright idea. She began to tap hurriedly at her computer.

Outside, a coach party of guests were disembarking and massing with their wheelie cases ready to descend on reception and check in.

Saskia wrote something on a scrap of paper and picked up her mobile phone.

'Hold fort!' she said, heading for the door.

'But I don't know the system....'

'Bullshit.'

Tracey wasn't sure whether this was supposed to be a comment or advice.

Either way Saskia wasn't listening. Tracey stood helplessly as the receptionist squeezed past the new arrivals and disappeared out of the hotel. Then she plastered a smile onto her face and prepared to greet them.

She got halfway through check-in before she got stuck. Then she turned to Naz. 'Precious,' she said, smiling sweetly over gritted teeth. 'Would you mind asking Gareth if he can sort out some complimentary drinks for these guests? And when you've done that, perhaps you could find Saskia for me and ask her if she's available to come back anytime soon?'

She turned back to the guests with the smile wilting but still just about intact. 'I'm so sorry, I seem to be having a slight problem with the computer. If you'd like to follow my colleague into the bar area, she'll arrange some refreshments for you while we sort it out.'

As soon as she could hand the guests over to Gareth, Naz headed outside. Storm clouds had gathered and were launching into a massive downpour. She hopped, skipped and jumped over and around the puddles in the uneven paving as rain lashed down all around her. In the flowerbeds the pale pink, straggling roses were flinching under the assault. The grounds at Horton Hill had never been the same since Whitlass sacked the old gardener and replaced him with his nephew. Naz remembered guiltily that she'd been meaning to find time to water these poor babies for days. The rain was saving her a job, though they didn't look very happy about it. The parched soil was flooding - as was the car park. Naz headed for the covered area by the van where most of the staff congregated to make phone calls.

She found Charlie having a crafty smoke, but there was no sign of Saskia. He said he thought he'd seen the receptionist going round the back of the hotel towards the old bicycle shelter. The 'bike shed', as it was affectionately called, had a good mobile signal and offered some cover for anyone wanting to make a private call without going back to their room. Since the Tour De France had descended on Yorkshire, some staff members had even started using it for bicycles again, and had been seen parading through the hotel lobby in very tight and very new Lycra outfits. Naz reckoned their enthusiasm was unlikely to survive a Yorkshire winter, though Saskia and Tracey were having a damned good laugh while it lasted.

As she got closer, Naz could hear a voice coming from the direction of the shelter. Its owner must have been talking loudly for it to carry through the clatter of the rain, so she guessed she was overhearing one side of a mobile phone call. The first few words were as meaningless as any random mobile talk might be.... 'Yes, we saw it in the paper.... Thank you so much for your help.... I will get the solicitor to phone you a.s.a.p. I hope you do not mind me ringing...'

Then came, 'No, I had the idea that you may not know that Kate was seeing Naz...' and Naz, suddenly furious at the idea of being gossiped about, found herself splashing round the corner to embarrass the culprit.

'Oh shit!' said Saskia as Naz careered into view.

'Bloody hell!' said Naz.

'I am really sorry, Mr Cohen,' said Saskia into the phone. 'I must talk to Naz about this now. Please will you let me know the minute there is any news?... Thank you *so* much... Yes... it is terrible business... I will bring her to speed now.... Thank you... Goodbye.'

'Your English is as good as mine!' gasped Naz as Saskia grabbed her by the back of her shirt and bundled her under the galvanised roof of the shelter.

'Shush!' she said. 'Is probably better in fact, but this is beside the point. I have no easy way to say this. The police arrested Kate today.'

'I have to go to London.' Naz's wet hair clung to her face and dripped down her neck. The colour had drained from her cheeks.

'Yes, you do... I know... And I will take you tomorrow.'

'I need to go now.'

This was what Saskia had feared. 'No,' she said firmly. 'You will not be able to see her anyway. I am going to sort out a solicitor and that is best thing for her now. If we go tomorrow I can get permission from Head Office. We can set off at 11am, miss the rush hour traffic and be there by mid-afternoon. Then we will do whatever it takes to get this pain-in-arse girlfriend out of the slammer. Okay?'

'Okay,' said Naz, acquiescing much more easily than Saskia had ever thought she would.

It was the shock, she thought, it had paralysed the kid. She gave her a stern look, just to make sure, but Naz looked miserable and beaten and quite passive. 'Poor Kate!' she said quietly, shaking her head.

'Okay... we have deal then.'

Somewhere through the shock, Naz remembered why she had come out to look for Saskia in the first place. 'Tracey's going nuts in there,' she said. 'She's got that coach party and she can't book them in.'

Saskia sighed. 'Okay, I will not be long. You go stall her while I make just two phone calls.'

'Alright,' said Naz. 'Thank you... But Saskia, why are you pretending to be foreign when you're not?'

'I *am* foreign,' said Saskia indignantly. 'And it is long story. I will tell it on way to London. But you must keep this secret for now... do you understand that?'

'What, even from Tracey?'

Saskia nodded gravely. 'Even from Tracey,' she said.

'Okay,' said Naz dully. 'Yes, I understand.'

Saskia lit a cigarette before she made her next phone call. It was in Slovak. In translation, it went something like this:

'Hey Mik!'

'Hi Sis.'

'We're good to go. I'll email the stuff across to you. As we suspected, he's been skimming cash off for a couple of years. The gardening, pool maintenance and even the money for last year's refurb... they've all gone to companies owned by friends and family of Mr Whitlass. Not to mention the computer upgrade. God knows where the new computers have gone, but they're not here. He's creamed thousands while the hotel's crumbling around him. The staff lift's a death trap. And that's before we even *start* on his minor bits of back door pilfering with his mate Max Pollack.'

'So, we've got him?' On the other end of the line, she heard her brother's little 'whoop' of excitement. It reminded her of when he was in short pants. She smiled at the memory.

'Yes. And I think the sooner we act now, the better. Is there any chance of you getting here tomorrow, first thing?' She knew he would. He was fresh from his Business Studies Degree and this was the first really big project his father had entrusted him with. He was desperate to get going with it.

'Wild horses wouldn't stop me! Do you think he'll go quietly?'

'He'd be a fool not to.... unless he likes prison food.'

'And do you think we can save the place? Truly?'

'I don't know. It's a mess. But the staff are good, in general, and there's a big regular clientele.... So maybe..... Don't get your hopes up too high though.'

'Okay. I'll get a better idea when I get there. It's going to be great to see you. You and me together, like the old days.'

Saskia crossed her fingers. 'Mik, I'm sorry,' she said. 'Something has come up in London and I need to get back there tomorrow. I was hoping I could use your flat.'

'But... I thought you might have stayed a day or two at least... to show me the ropes.'

She could hear the disappointment in his voice. It tore at her heart. 'I'm sorry Mikulas, but Tracey and Lucinda will be able to show you everything you need to know.'

'Ah... Tracey.... The girl with the red hair.'

He knew the staff (*his* staff as he saw them now) by heart.

Saskia noticed he didn't pick up on her mention of Lucinda. She wondered if he thought she was too much a part of the old regime to be trusted. That would be a shame, as she was actually a good worker and could be an asset to a revitalised Horton Hill. She decided it wasn't any of her business anymore though. This was Mik's project now. 'Yes, Tracey's good.... Stroppy... but good. You'll like her.' From what Saskia knew of his taste in women, she thought he might like her rather too much. But he was old enough to sort out his own love life too.

'And Naz.... the girl who ticks three of our Equal Opportunities boxes in one go... You told me *she* was very good...'

Despite herself, Saskia smiled. 'Mik... when did you turn into our father?'

He laughed. 'When he made me a company director.'

'Well, I want my little brother back please. And actually, you'll need to manage without Naz too for a few days. I have to take her to London with me.'

'How come?'

'Her girlfriend's been arrested for murder and we need to sort things out.'

There was a long silence as Mikulas digested this.

Finally, he laughed. 'Hah!' he said. 'You almost had me there..... Hey... Are you two..?'

'No...' said Saskia hastily. 'God, no!' It had never crossed her mind that her feelings for Naz were anything other than friendship. The idea sat uneasily with her now.

'It's cool with me if you are. It might even be better for you. You always had such lousy taste in men!'

'Well thank you for that Mik!' It was embarrassing to think that her love life was such an obvious disaster that even her little brother had noticed. 'But we're not.'

'Oh well. Maybe it's for the best. Dad would have gone ape-shit!'

'Might be worth it just for that then,' said Saskia drily. She was glad that he couldn't see the blush slowly creeping up her neck and into her cheeks. 'But anyway, I'm straight and she's in love with someone else, so it's not going to happen.'

'Okay. Well, I'll give her a week off, just because it's you. But you'll have to get her back to work then, or I'll replace her.'

'Mik, you're all heart!'

'Actually, I'm *way* too soft.'

'Well, that's good isn't it?'

'No,' he growled, but she could hear the smile in his voice. 'In business soft is *not* good. How can you be in our family, and not know that?'

She hung up. Dialled again... 'Auntie Anna?'

'My God, Saskia. I thought you were dead. You never phone... you never write...'

'Hah hah!'

'And now, I'm sure you must want something, because you are phoning your old Teta Anna.'

Saskia waited for her aunt to stop chortling down the phone.

'Yes... you've sussed me,' she said. 'I need a good criminal lawyer. And, of course, I thought of you....'

Despite the evidence, Jamila struggled to see Kate as a cold blooded murderer. She looked so frightened it was hard not to want to reach across to comfort her. But they were in an interview room now and the tape was running. Peter was by her side in professional copper mode and Anna Maxwell, the sharp-witted, fiery tempered and often highly controversial defence lawyer had replaced the duty solicitor and was facing them across the table. Jamila had only come across Anna a couple of times before. She tended to work on the kind of high profile cases that hit the news and went on forever. Rock stars, politicians, company moguls... The CPS hated her because she usually won. Jamila wondered how on earth Kate was able to afford her.

Pete was plodding through the evidence in his steady, thorough, emotionless way.

He put stills from the Pay and Display CCTV on the table, slowly, nudging each one towards her as he referred to it.... Friday 6th June 11.25pm.... Friday 13th June 11.50pm.... Friday 20th June 11.43pm... Is this your car?'

Kate's eyes wouldn't focus, and the images were fuzzy anyway. 'I.. I don't know,' she said... 'It could be...'

Peter showed her a close-up of the registration plate.

'Yes,' said Kate, shakily. 'Yes, it is.'

'And is this you?' he pointed to the figure locking the car door.

'It can't be. I was in bed.'

'Alone?'

'Yes.'

'And you say that no-one has car keys except you.'

'Not that I know of.'

'And no-one has keys to your flat except you.'

Kate shook her head.

'Is that a "no"?'

'I've never given anyone else a key to my flat.'

'So what about these?' He placed six photographs down in front of her. They appeared to be more images of her locking the car and crossing the street but they were from a different angle, as if they had been taken from an upstairs window across the street and slightly above.

'I don't know...'

'They came from an envelope we found in the filing cabinet at your flat. The originals are in this phone....' He nudged the mobile towards her. 'Could you explain how it came to be in your possession?'

'No.'

'Well maybe, you could explain these text messages we found in the "Sent" folder of this phone... "I wish I could be with you now"... "I only feel truly alive with you"... "I can't wait to see you again"...'

Kate blinked. In the cold light of day, she knew how they sounded. 'I thought she was struggling with being alone. She told me she'd never lived alone before. She was traumatised and frightened.'

'Not in love with you then?'

'You don't have to answer that,' said Anna, to Kate. 'You've already given a perfectly good explanation.'

'No,' said Kate. 'I want to answer that.... I *don't* think she was in love with me.'

'Isn't that fairly standard though... clients falling in love with their therapists?'

'Not in the model I use.'

'Oh?... So what about these later texts? What about "Where are you now when I need you?" "I feel like I'm too much for you." "What we did was wrong." "What we did was really bad. I feel so used."'

'I have no idea. I was going to talk to her about them at her next appointment, but she was ill.'

'So you took her home?'

'Yes.'

'And put her to bed?'

'She put herself to bed.'

'You left her in bed.'

'Yes.' Kate seemed to be shrinking under his questioning.

'My client showed basic human compassion to someone who was ill,' said Anna, 'I hardly think that can be classed as a crime.'

'Is this your diazepam?'

'Yes.'

'Can you explain to me again how it came to be in your bathroom cabinet?'

'I told you before. My GP prescribes it to me for anxiety.'

'Isn't that a bit odd? A therapist who needs to resort to tranquillisers to manage anxiety?'

'Yes, I guess so.' Jamila saw Kate's shoulders droop in shame.

'Did you give tranquillisers to this client?'

'Certainly not.'

'Could she have taken them from your bathroom?'

'Yes, she went to the bathroom that day.'

'Did you tell her she could take them?'

'No, of course not!'

Anna looked up lazily from the A4 pad she was doodling on. 'Diazepam is a very commonly prescribed tranquilliser,' she said.

'But there is no record of Rachel Ryder ever being prescribed it.'

Anna looked down again... continued doodling.

'Tell me about *these* photographs.' Laclan dealt four in front of Kate with the precision of a croupier in a casino.

Jamila heard her sharp intake of breath and saw the small amount of colour she'd retained draining out of her face. She looked at the photos again, herself. Colour prints of Rachel striking the kind of poses teenage boys might have looked at in top shelf magazines before the internet came along and saved them the embarrassment of going into a real shop. She imagined they must be the same kind of images Mike Ryder had found on Rachel's computer and phone. The images she'd sent to Jed Watkins to masturbate over.

'Or maybe these...?' He dealt another four and held the rest, as if he could keep going for some time.

Kate's hands had gone up to her mouth. Jamila wondered if she might actually be about to be sick.

'I... I've never seen them before...' she stammered.

'Well, that's odd Kate, because they seem to have been taken in your bedroom... This *is* your bedroom isn't it..? This *is* your bed...? We're checking the forensics of course, but I would say they're likely to make interesting reading.'

Kate still seemed stunned. Jamila felt that she was on the verge of saying something.

Maybe Anna Maxwell sensed it too because she stood up. 'I would like to speak with my client alone,' she said.

Laclan ignored her. 'It's best to tell the truth Kate,' he said, looking her straight in the eyes. 'Did you have sex with Rachel Ryder?'

Anna put her hand on Kate's arm to silence her. She glared down at Laclan. 'I **said** I would like to speak with my client alone. I expect you to respect that!'

Naz was completely wired that night. She stayed up as late as she could. She tried to concentrate on her work and couldn't. Then she tried to sleep and she couldn't do that either. In the early hours she downloaded the Sam Smith song Kate had played at her flat the only day they had ever truly spent together. But it didn't really help her very much. It was sad. She didn't like the bit about it not being love. And it made her want to cry.

At night, the police cells were alive with noise - singing, screaming, shouting, swearing – a turbulent, angry cacophony of protest and pleading that created an almost operatic backdrop to Kate's inner turmoil. Panic crashed through her in waves. It felt like the emotional equivalent of being lashed to a ship's mast in a storm, battered until she thought she would drown, then gulping for air as the ship rose, only to topple dizzily down the far side and into the next wave and the next. She remembered Naz in the lift, how they had sung together and she'd felt better. Anna Maxwell, the lawyer who had suddenly appeared from nowhere to replace the tired and rather burnt-out looking duty solicitor, had told her that Naz was coming to London, was desperate to see her as soon as she could. But she couldn't find comfort in that. She daren't bring herself to imagine anything in the future anymore. She tried to remember the words of the song, but it didn't help. None of her strategies worked in this place. They were designed for lesser worries, things that seemed trivial now. But they were powerless here where her guilt ran screaming through the hallways, denouncing her, saying that this was no more than she deserved, that she'd been getting away with it for years and now she was exposed for what she truly was, at last. It hardly seemed to matter that she couldn't have done what they accused her of, was incapable of killing anyone, even Rachel Stiles. The feeling was the same and it would have been a relief to be able to say it out loud to someone. But she knew that she couldn't because her crime had been committed years ago and now the only other person who knew about it was dead.

All around, the noise continued unabated. She pushed herself into the corner of the bed with her back against the wall, and stared into the gloom ahead of her, re-running her guilt over and over in her mind. It was a cold and lonely re-running. Never any comfort in it, only blame and self loathing. But she did it anyway. She couldn't help herself. It was as if the thing had come to have a life of its own.

When Dick Whitlass arrived for work the next morning, he opened his office door to find a strange young man sitting in his swivel-chair. There was a cardboard box on the desk. The framed photograph of himself in his student days, shaking hands with Margaret Thatcher, was clearly visible in there, along with several executive toys, a half eaten pack of chocolate digestives, and the grubby slippers he sometimes surreptitiously wore when he was having his afternoon nap.

'Who the hell are *you*?' he spluttered, outraged at this invasion of his domain.

The sharp-suited young man stood and nudged the box towards him.

'I am the owner of this hotel,' he said. 'And *you* are fired.'

It was said that Lucinda's scream of shock and grief could be heard in every corner of the hotel. Certainly, it brought guests running into the lobby. Mikulas would have liked to send her home to consider whether she still had a future at Horton Hill. But he couldn't, because two of his key workers were about to head for London. He was relieved that he'd had the foresight to contact a Temp Agency in Leeds as soon as he'd realised that Saskia was running out on him. And he was enjoying the adrenalin rush of it all. He figured it was time now to get the delectable Tracey into his office and come up with a plan of action for the next few days.

Tracey was outside with Saskia and Naz. She'd been struggling to keep her Breakfast Team focused all morning as rumours flew back and forth between the kitchen and front of house staff. When Lucinda's meltdown had heralded the news of Whitlass's demise, and Charlie ran to lock himself in the loo for fear of being next, she'd almost given up, but she'd held everyone to their posts, and only now, when the last guest had left the breakfast room, had she let them out to gossip and exchange increasingly colourful versions of the morning's events.

At first, when she spotted her two friends packing their cases into Saskia's battered blue Fiesta, she was fearful that they'd been given the push too, and wondered if Jason had dobbed Naz in after all about the van incident. But now she'd realised that they were, actually, going to try to sort out Naz's girlfriend problems, she was telling them, in no uncertain terms, how she felt about being abandoned. 'So, you think it's okay to just bugger off and leave me to the tender mercies of this new boss?' she demanded.

'I'm sorry. It's just... I've got to see Kate... I'll be back as soon as I can.'

'Pffuhh!!!!' Tracey wasn't in the mood for excuses. 'And *you're* not even foreign!' she added, glowering accusingly at Saskia.

'Yes I am!' Saskia protested.

'Hardly!' snorted Tracey. 'You're a mole from Head Office.'

'Well, was worth it, no? To nail Whitlass? Is amazing what people will discuss in hearing when they think you not understand them.'

'That's beside the point.' Her lip jutted out. 'Just what the hell am I going to do without you both?'

Saskia was surprised to see tears in her friend's eyes as she came towards her for a hug. She felt herself freeze involuntarily, as she always did when people came too close. She patted stiffly at Tracey's back. 'Will come visit,' she said gruffly.

'You'd bloody better!' Tracey sniffed and turned to hug Naz. 'And if you move to London to live with Katie Bleedin' Ferrings it'll be *me* that's sent down for murder – right?'

Mikulas had been watching the scene for some time before he cleared his throat.

'You must be Tracey,' he said. 'I would like to have you in my office.'

She turned and her eyes swept over his skilfully ruffled black hair and deep-set brown eyes. She knew that his suit was Paul Smith and his watch, Montblanc. She'd never seen anyone quite like him, even when she worked at Rodley Grange. She thought he was gorgeous. Her tears dried instantly.

'Well – 'bye then,' she said cheerily over her shoulder to her two friends as she followed him, mesmerized, into the hotel.

Mikulas turned at the main entrance and waved to his sister. 'Ďakujem,' he mouthed.

'You're welcome,' she replied.

In the car, Naz was fretting about Kate. 'So, we're going straight to Mr Cohen's flat?' she asked, checking the arrangements for the third time. 'Have you got the address in your Sat Nav?'

'No. I thought I would go by direction of the sun.'

'Oh hah hah... Very funny. Seriously though, *have* you?' It was hard to tell, since the Sat Nav was speaking to them in Slovak.

'Do not worry,' said Saskia. 'Take deep breath.' Naz noticed that the quality of Saskia's English varied in direct proportion to how much she was concentrating on it. While she was driving she had almost reverted to the old familiar Saskia-speak she knew so well. It felt reassuring.

'I'm sorry,' she said. 'It's just... I know how much she'll hate being locked up.'

'Yes. It is not good. Mind if I smoke?.... I will put the window down.'

Smoke billowed around Naz, blown across the car by the side-draught from the motorway.

It reminded her of Jess and her shame.

'Have you ever got drunk and done something *really* stupid?' she asked.

'First rule of drinking,' said Saskia, inhaling deeply. 'Always have enough to wipe out all memory. It is for the best. You have much to learn about the ways of the world young Nazzaro.'

Naz wondered if that was how her mother had stumbled into alcoholism. She doubted whether she'd ever catch her sober enough to have a sensible conversation about it though.

She tried to put Jess out of her mind.

'Maybe Kate will have already been released when we get there,' she said hopefully.

'Perhaps.' Saskia tried to inject an upbeat tone into her voice as she said this, though in truth, she didn't feel particularly hopeful after her text exchange with her Aunt Anna that morning. An extension to police questioning-time never boded well in her experience. She'd been selective in how much she had shared with Naz about this though.

And the optimistic tone seemed to have done the trick.

'So, how did you come to end up on covert ops at Horton Hill?' asked Naz, finally pulling her thoughts away from Kate long enough to get interested in something else.

'Are you sure you would like to know?'

'Yes!' Naz liked to immerse herself in other people's lives. She'd learnt to do it when she was very small and both her mum and Nan were off their heads most of the time. Coronation Street had been a favourite source of information about how other people might live. Though the Milton family next door, with their picnics and Trivial Pursuit at Christmas, had come a close second. 'Okay.' Saskia tossed her cigarette butt out of the window and closed it, turning up the air conditioning. 'When I was nine, my father inherited KV Hospitality Industries from his Great Uncle Radek in Seattle. Before then, Father had simply been hotel manager in Bratislava. He was never a nice man. But we were happy because he was working all the time and so we rarely saw him. I have two brothers, Bronislav, who is older, and Mikulas, who you met this morning, who is three years younger than me.'

'So... you're actually the new boss's sister?' Naz was struggling to rearrange the pieces of this particular jigsaw. 'And the Big Boss's daughter...'

'Yes!'

'Blimey!....Tracey's going to be *well* pissed off when she finds out!'

'I know!... Anyway, my mother is very beautiful person, very kind and very pretty. My brothers inherited her good-looks, but sadly, I look like my father. The money was not good for him. It went to his head and turned him into an arrogant arse-hole. When I was eleven, he traded Mother in for a very much younger model and I was sent to Boarding School in UK, where my father believed I would be polished into a beautiful English/Slovakian rose. Once there I discovered that I must learn English quickly or die of drowning with my head down the toilet pan. Indeed "No, please, do not put my head in the toilet," was the first English phrase I learnt... When I left school with no GCSEs but an encyclopaedic knowledge of designer drugs and secret ways into the boy's school, I tried to make my own way in the world. But sadly, I have talent for nothing, so I gave in to my fate, joined the family 'firm' and here I am!'

Naz thought it was sad how much the real Saskia put herself down. She wondered what had happened to the feisty receptionist they'd left behind.

'Well, *I* think you're talented' she said. 'You were great at your job at Horton Hill. Everybody loved you there.'

'Being rude to people by pretending not to understand them is not the same as being great at job,' said Saskia. 'Though I admit, it was good fun!' When she thought about her time 'undercover' she realised she had been happier during those few weeks than she had been for years..... Much happier, in fact, than she had ever been since her father's unexpected windfall had torn her away from all her friends and blown her family apart.

'Yeah.... But people really liked you. You have a lovely smile. You made them feel welcome. Even Kate, when she was in such a bad mood and you were winding her up with the tango thing... you took her mind off her problems.' Hah... there she was, back to Kate again. There was no doubt that this girl was in love.

'Did I?'

'Yeah! You shouldn't put yourself down so much. I think you're really pretty and you're a great friend. Just look at what you're doing for me now... That's really special. I reckon you take after your mum a lot more than you think.'

Saskia *knew* that she was a good friend. She put herself out for people. It was one of her strongest personal values. Though sometimes, when she was feeling particularly insecure, she told herself she only did it to buy people's friendship. The 'pretty' thing, however, was news to her.

'You think I'm *pretty*?' she found herself blushing as she asked this. And she felt embarrassed that she wanted it confirmed.

'Yes, I do.'

She laughed, to hide her pleasure at hearing it. 'Then, I'm sorry, young Nazzaro,' she said, lighting up another cigarette and rolling the window down again. 'I think you should have gone to Specsavers.'

David Cohen was having a bad day.

First the news that Kate's detention at the police station had been extended.

Then that 'insufferable prick' (as he'd called him the minute he'd hung up the phone) Jim Crowe, calling to stick the knife into Kate.... 'Reflects badly on the Institute, David... Think we need to distance ourselves from her... suspend her membership until all this is cleared up...'

And now the phone had just rung again and David resisted the very strong temptation to let it go straight to voicemail. As soon as he heard Anna Maxwell's firm voice on the other end of the line, he wished he had. 'This is not good,' she said. 'There is a lot of evidence against your friend.'

David took a deep breath, along with a gulp of the red wine he'd just poured himself when he still believed the worst of the day was over. 'But *you* believe she's innocent, don't you?' he asked, helplessly.

'Of course, I'm her lawyer. It's my job to believe that.'

And it was David's job to listen to what lay beneath people's words. He knew she thought Kate was guilty.

'What do we do now?' he asked, almost beaten.

'I'll send someone round,' she said.

Then she was gone.

The "someone" was a tall young woman with short, almost white, blonde hair, gelled into spikes. She wore pale blue jeans and a thin pastel-striped top with a scoop neck. She introduced herself as Jaiden Brady, and there was something reassuringly confident about the way she shook David's hand.

'Anna thought she needed to call in the cavalry,' she said.

David found himself smiling for the first time in days. 'And that's you?'

'Absolutely!... Have you got anything cool to drink? I've just come on the bus and I'm *gasping*!'

By the time Saskia and Naz arrived, Jaiden was ensconced in David's fireside chair, sipping lager (with ice) from a tall glass. She stood up as David showed the new arrivals into the room.

'You must be Naz... and I'm guessing you're Saskia.' She'd done her homework and she held out her hand to each of them in turn. She sized them up quickly. The younger woman was pretty and cute in an unassuming sort of a way. She was also, obviously, deeply distressed. Saskia was much more interesting - curvy, soft, a 'proper' woman, in Jaiden's book. 'Your Auntie Anna says you must see her while you're in London,' she said.

'Yes. I will phone her tonight to arrange something.'

Naz noticed that Saskia's English was now perfect again. It was quite an achievement after their long and tiring drive on the motorway followed by a, frankly, terrifying rat-run through the streets of Outer London.

'Let me get you something to drink.' David was digesting the news that the solicitor was Saskia's aunt. She hadn't mentioned *that* when she gave him the number. It explained the bluntness though. It was obviously a family trait. 'I've got some red wine open... or there's lager in the fridge...'

Jaiden raised her glass. He assumed that this was a sign of recommendation, though actually, she was hinting for a top-up.

'Or maybe a nice cup of tea or coffee, or a soft drink? I don't keep anything like Coke, I'm afraid, but I've got some non-alcoholic ginger beer.'

He thinks I'm a kid, thought Naz.

I could murder a double vodka, thought Saskia.

'A cup of tea would be nice,' they both said, out loud.

David hurried off into the kitchen and left Jaiden to update them. He told himself it was cowardly, but he really couldn't cope with being the bearer of more bad news right now.

When he returned with the tea, the three women were sitting in silence. Naz looked close to tears, Saskia was glaring at his antique Persian rug as if it had offended her in some way, and Jaiden was about an inch away from emptying her glass. He took it into the kitchen and filled it again for her.

'I need a cigarette,' she said, decisively, as he came back. 'Thanks David, I'll take that with me.' She reached for the condensation beaded glass and headed for the door.

'Me too!' Saskia leapt to her feet and followed her out of the room with one of his best china teacups rattling precariously on its saucer as she went.

Naz had tucked herself into the corner of David's sofa. She slurped miserably at her tea and stayed put. Looking at her, David realised just how tired he was of spending all his time comforting people in distress. Maybe that was another reason he'd allowed Kate to push herself so hard. She'd seemed like someone who might be keen to take over his insatiable sense of responsibility for the world.

He forced himself into autopilot.

'Guess we're the boring non-smokers then,' he said kindly, pouring himself another glass of wine and sitting down beside her.

'It's going to be so awful for her in prison,' said Naz and then, as he'd feared, she began to cry.

'So... can Auntie Anna get her off the hook?'

They were standing on the stone steps at the front of the house with their drinks perched on the window ledge beside them. The tiny garden looked sadly neglected, despite its low maintenance design – a circular patch of crazy paving with a sundial on a plinth, surrounded by bushes of French Lavender, Rosemary and Potentilla. Saskia noticed that there was a weathered Twix wrapper in the hedge, and a scattering of cigarette butts on the soil where incoming clients had smoked last cigarettes before their sessions. It smelt nice though, and the late afternoon air was warm after yesterday's rain.

Jaiden licked the paper of her roll-up and pulled a straggle of tobacco out of the end.

'She's frustrated.' She clicked her lighter and held it to the tip of Saskia's Marlborough before lighting her own altogether lumpier creation. 'She thinks Kate's hiding something from her.'

'Like what?' Saskia inhaled deeply then blew a long, slim stream of smoke into the air, raising her chin slightly as if she were aiming at the sky. The smell of smoke obliterated the lavender.

'Hard to say.... something inappropriate with the client probably... Though I'm not gonna say that in front of the girlfriend, obviously.'

'Mm… better not. Though they have not been together for very long.'

'Thing is.... If only she'd admit to something like that, Anna could probably go for manslaughter, or even accidental death. But all this, "It wasn't her", "I wasn't there," "I didn't do it"... It just doesn't wash when they've got Kate's dabs all over the murder scene, her car on CCTV, the victim's DNA and fingerprints (inevitably... they're just waiting for forensics) in her bedroom... plus Rachel's mobile phone and a whole wodge of saucy photos that were definitely taken at Kate's place, stashed away at the back of her filing cabinet.'

Saskia gazed up at the sky, screwing her eyes up slightly to watch the high white clouds basking in the intensity of the blue. 'Yeah,' she said. 'She has been stitched up like kipper and no mistake.'

Jaiden thought Saskia and Naz were likely to be a bit overwhelming for Kate's beleaguered parents. So she left them in 'The Flying Horseman', a Gastro Pub five minutes away from the respectable North London street where Kate had grown up, and headed purposefully towards Number 23 with David by her side.

'Remember we need to keep focused,' she said. 'We're looking for someone with a grudge against both Kate and Rachel. And bearing in mind that they seem to have hated each other's guts, anybody fitting that particular bill should stand out like a drag queen at a dyke's ball.'

'Okay,' David nodded. He felt out of his depth, and if he'd known that he'd be called upon to play detective that evening he certainly would never have started on the red wine.

Jaiden noticed his discomfort. 'Just think of them as clients,' she said.

He wasn't sure whether that felt better – or worse.

The warm smell of honeysuckle in full flower wafted from the hedge as he opened the gate. It took him back suddenly, achingly, to the first flat he'd ever bought with Daniel. The unruly fronds around their front door had always seemed to need pruning just when they were at their heaviest with fragrant pink and yellow blooms. He'd never got the hang of the plant – or of gardening either, for that matter. But the scent reminded him so strongly of those happier days that he found himself struggling to hold back tears.

'Mr Ferrings?' Jaiden's voice jolted him back to the present, and he forced himself to focus on the grey haired man in white shirt and grey flannel trousers who had just opened the door. He bore, David could see, the familiar tell-tale stare of someone in the midst of trauma.

'We spoke on the phone,' Jaiden continued. 'This is David, a friend of Kate's.'

'Well actually, I'm her superv.....' David began, then stopped, realising that circumstances had, in a strange kind of way, made Jaiden's description more accurate.

Mr Ferrings half waited for him to finish the sentence, then gave up with a shrug. 'Her mother is in bits,' he said, and gestured for them to come in.

God, he looks so *old*, thought David.... Old, and heartbroken.

They followed him through a narrow hallway with a mirror and coat hooks, into a small, sunny sitting room dominated by the upright piano against its far wall.

Mrs Ferrings stood painfully to greet them. David noticed that her legs were red and swollen. She supported herself on sticks. 'Mr Cohen,' she said. 'I'm so pleased to meet you. Our daughter thinks the world of you. It would be a great comfort to her to know that you've come here to see us today.'

When they'd been served with tea and home baked fruit cake, carried in from the kitchen by Mr Ferrings, Jaiden gave the anxious parents a heavily censored run-down of the evidence against Kate.

They listened gravely. Then her mother said what she had obviously wanted to say all along. 'Kathryn never could have done this, you know. She doesn't have it in her.'

Jaiden nodded sympathetically. She'd read the notes, and she didn't see Kate as a cold-blooded killer either. Though in truth, she still wasn't convinced that she hadn't killed her tormentor by accident. She wasn't about to express that particular theory in front of the distraught parents though. Not at this stage, at least.

'I agree,' she said carefully and kindly. 'But if Kate's innocent... as I'm sure she is.... It's very clear that someone has deliberately set out to incriminate her... Can you think of anyone who might dislike her enough to want to do that?'

They both shook their heads – their eyes big and childlike as they looked at her.

Jaiden tried a different tack; 'Do you know much about her relationship with Rachel Stiles?'

This clearly hit a nerve with her mother. 'Rachel was a horrible girl!' she said. 'She was spoilt and nasty. She bullied poor Kate... Rachel and those other two... Julie and Sally.... Even Sally's own grandma despairs of her. I used to try to encourage Kate to "turn the other cheek" but I wondered if that just made her more of a target.'

'Hard to see how it wouldn't,' said David. He came from more of an 'eye for an eye' background himself and, even as a gay man, he'd never had any problems with bullies.

Mrs Ferrings looked at him. 'It's our faith,' she said, simply.

Instantly, he felt chided and a little bit ashamed. 'Yes... of course... I'm sorry.'

Jaiden stepped in to smooth ruffled feathers. 'That's Julie Groves and Sally Ballantree?' she clarified.

'Yes. Nasty girls. They used to reduce poor Kate to tears with their spitefulness.'

Jaiden nodded again, as if she were hearing this for the first time.

'Rachel's husband said that he thought Kate and Rachel were quite friendly at one time.'

Mrs Ferrings bridled at this. 'Rubbish! Our daughter would never associate with a Godless little trollop like that!'

Jaiden shrugged. 'He must have been mistaken then,' she said smoothly. 'I guess he wouldn't have really known what went on between the girls.... Did Kate have any other friends who might have had any inside understanding of how things were for Kate back then?'

Mrs Ferrings looked hopeful. 'There's Sue,' she said. 'Kate's best friend. They've always been very close.'

'Sue?.... She hasn't mentioned her.'

'No. She'll be trying not to get her involved. Her nerves aren't good. But she'll want to help if she can, I'm sure.'

If Jaiden was excited by the emergence of this new witness, she didn't show it. 'Do you have a number for her?' she asked casually.

They looked at each other. They didn't seem like the sort of couple who would be very good on the phone.

'No, but we always send her a Christmas card. She lives on a houseboat near Richmond, with her friend, Brenda.... Desmond... get the address book will you?'

Mr Ferrings walked them to the gate.

'There's something else,' he said, glancing behind him to make sure his wife was still in the house and couldn't hear. 'I don't know whether it might be important or not.'

'It's surprising what can turn out to be important,' said Jaiden reassuringly.

He nodded. 'It's just that when Kate was sixteen, we... her mother and myself... we went to a Church Prayer Weekend... and Susan stayed here with Kate. I've never said anything about it to Mrs Ferrings, but I always thought something happened that weekend... something that really upset both of them. Whatever you do, you mustn't breathe a word of this to my wife, but I always wondered if they may have had some boys round. There were some signs that our bed had been.... slept in. Sue had her first breakdown shortly after that, and Kate was never the same either, to be honest.'

Jaiden rewarded him with a smile. 'Thank you Mr Ferrings,' she said. 'I'm sure that will be very helpful.... When you say that Sue had her first breakdown... what form did that take?'

There was a long silence as Kate's father struggled with what he could and couldn't say.

A car drove past. Two neighbours walked by, probably on their way to the pub. They greeted Mr Ferrings. David wondered if they'd read the newspapers and knew about Kate. He imagined that her father was wondering that too. Mrs Ferrings had come to the window and was looking out at them. And standing there, enveloped once more, in the heartbreaking scent of the honeysuckle, he realised that apart from his religious faux pas, he'd barely said a word throughout the whole interview.

Kate's father ran an exhausted hand over his eyes. He looked too old to be dealing with this kind of upset. 'She tried to kill herself,' he said. 'And if our Kate hadn't found her, she probably would have succeeded too.'

Jaiden put her hand on his arm as if she were steadying him. 'It's going to be okay,' she said, and he looked up into her eyes, trustingly, relieved to have handed over a responsibility that had always been too big for him. 'Do you really think so?'

'Yes... I'm sure of it....' She paused, and David could see her thinking, looking at all the angles, sizing everything up. For a moment, he thought she'd finished, that they would just take their leave now and go. But there was just one box she hadn't ticked, so she kept her hand on the old man's arm. 'You probably can't remember this,' she said. 'It was a long time ago. But...'

He interrupted her. 'Can I remember the date?... Yes, of course I can... It was the weekend of the 21st and 22nd October 2,000. I remember it exactly because that was the weekend I lost my daughter.'

By the time they left The Flying Horseman, they all knew their roles for the following day.

'Okay...' said Jaiden. 'Any chance of a lift home for me and David?'

'Of course,' said Saskia stoically.

'Good, well I'll check out the internet chatter tonight. Reckon people will be turning Facebook and Twitter red hot about this. We'll reconvene back at David's tomorrow at 4pm, right?'

'Right!' they chorused.

None of them felt particularly upbeat.

But it was good to have something useful to do at least.

Saskia and Naz got to Mikulas's apartment at just after 9pm.

Saskia punched the code into the burglar alarm. 'God, it has been a long day!' Relieved of driving duties at last, she searched in the kitchen cupboard for vodka and poured a hefty measure into a thick bottomed glass. 'Want?' she asked Naz.

'No thanks.' The apartment had huge windows with spectacular views across the Thames towards the MI5 building. The sky was darkening and the lights of London were starting to dot across the city. Naz was standing by the window, looking out at the river below. 'This is so beautiful,' she said.

'Yes.' Saskia came to stand beside her, breathing in the view and realising that until she had noticed her brother's king size bed, she hadn't given any thought at all to the issue of sleeping arrangements. 'I see why Mikulas loves it here,' she said. She could almost convince herself that her wistful mood was purely for London and its magnificent skyline.... almost... but not quite. Inwardly, she cursed Mik for putting this idea of loving Naz into her mind. 'And I must phone Auntie Anna.' Maybe, if she distracted herself for long enough, the thought would start to seem silly again, as it had the first time she'd heard it. She took herself away to make the call.

At Horton Hill, Tracey was stacking chairs in the breakfast room ready to mop the floor. Mikulas had been watching her from the lobby. Now he came to the doorway and called in to her. 'Have you finished?'

'Not quite.'

'I'll help you.' He slung his jacket on one of the tables and took the mop and bucket.

'I think I need to come clean with you about Saskia,' he said. 'I know that the two of you have become good friends.'

Her heart sank. 'Are you...?' she couldn't bring herself to say the word, she wanted him too much.

'Yes.'

'I should have known.'

'I don't see why. It isn't as if we *look* anything like each other.'

'I'm sorry?'

'Well, everyone says she looks more like our father.'

There was a long pause as she recalculated. Relief swept through her as two and two finally made four. 'She's your *sister*?'

'Yes.... what did you think I meant?'

'It doesn't matter!' She laughed as she shook her head, so relieved she even forgot to be angry with Saskia for deceiving her.

'She was the only one I could trust to do this,' he said.

'Well, she made a bloody good job of it!'

'Maybe she could have a new career on the stage.'

'Or in the Secret Service!'

'Yeah,' he was smiling too now at the idea. He pretended to blow on the end of a gun. 'The name's Blonde...' he intoned. 'Saskia Blonde!'

'Well, that would frighten *me*!' Tracey smiled, feeling his eyes searching for hers as he laughed.

'I used to do this for my father when I was a boy in Bratislava,' he said, going back to his mopping. 'He said I did it very well.'

'You do.' Her heart melted as she watched him. 'I feel bad, standing here and watching you work.'

'I don't see why. I've been standing there and watching *you* for a long time.' He gestured to the lobby where his relief receptionist was quietly booking in some late arrivals. 'And I wondered if you would like to have a drink with me before bed.'

He noticed how her hand stroked her throat as she watched him. He wanted her to stroke him like that.

'I should warn you that all the optics in the bar are watered,' she said.

'I'll change them in the morning. I have a bottle of fine brandy in my room.' He picked up the mop and bucket. 'Where should I take this?'

His eyes deepened as he waited for her response.

'I'll show you,' she said. Then suddenly serious, she added. 'Look, be honest with me. Are you a nice guy or a bastard? It doesn't matter in a way. It's just that if you're a bastard I'd like to be prepared, that's all.'

'I *can* be a bit of a bastard,' said Mikulas.

'Okay, just so long as I know.'

'But my sister will probably kill me if I'm a bastard to *you.*'

Jamila hadn't seen much point in going home early that night. With Sayed at a dinner with potential clients and not due home till after midnight, it felt only natural to get in the obligatory cappuccinos and settle down beside Peter at his desk.

'Anna Maxwell's put Jaiden on the Kate Ferrings case,' he said, swinging his chair round to reach for his cup.

'Gosh. Isn't that a bit risky?'

'Well, if anyone can get to the bottom of this, *she* can.'

'Yes, but is anything she digs out likely to be admissible?'

Peter smiled, remembering Jaiden's rather turbulent and short-lived career at 'The Met'... 'I think she's learnt her lesson on *that* score,' he said, though, actually, he doubted it. 'By the way, do we have any idea who's been tipping the press off about this one?'

Jamila raised her eyebrows. 'Do we ever? Someone who doesn't care how many people's lives they ruin, as usual.'

They sipped in silence for a while, both enjoying the quiet and the companionship.

'How come you're still here?' asked Jamila eventually.

'I could ask the same of you.'

'Yes... but I asked first.'

He sighed. 'Because I'm a lonely old sod. And I couldn't face the microwave lasagne that seemed like a good idea when it was part of a 'Buy One Get One Free' offer at the supermarket a few days back.... Now you....?'

'Sayed's out and it's a big house when I'm on my own.'

Laclan nodded sympathetically. 'All houses are big when you're on your own,' he said, with feeling.

Kate wondered if the long hours in her police cell were acting like a kind of 'psychological flooding' - washing away old terrors like a river bursting its banks and tearing away everything in its path. Though actually, the rational part of her knew that her slight sense of detachment was much more likely to be down to the diazepam the police doctor had finally allowed her, than to any positive result of being locked up for thirty plus hours with only her claustrophobia, Laclan and Shah and the mysteriously appointed Anna Maxwell for company.

It seemed ironic that the tranquilliser that had felt like her best friend right now had proved to be a major player in the death of her worst enemy. She wondered about the role of karma in it all. Maybe, finally, this was payback time. It certainly felt as if Rachel, who, after all, knew exactly what she'd done, was mocking her, even in death. And despite all the horror of it, this was a strangely comforting thought. As if something, finally, might be resolved.

She remembered, huddled there in the corner of her cell, how Susan, had first appeared, with her mother and younger sister at the 'Church Of The Road To The Cross' where Kate's mum was the pianist. It was the August of Kate's sixteenth birthday and the small family had looked hesitant enough to turn tail and run as they entered the modern Church Hall just before the Sunday service.

They'd had a battered look about them – new to the area, shy, and probably drawn more by the promise of making friends than any hope of finding God.

The 'Church of the Road' was big on friendliness. It had a billboard outside with messages like: 'What's Missing from CH—CH?' and 'Jesus was child-friendly – So are we!', and its Pastor, Eli Brown, had always set out to provide a warm welcome and hot cups of tea to the lost, the lonely and the downtrodden.

As a child, attending Sunday School, Kate had loved the place... The ancient box of Fuzzy Felt Bible Stories with lions for Daniel's den, only two wise men and no donkey;

church picnics and carol services; and the great songs, a bit like Naz's 'Born to Be Wild', with actions like marching 'with the infantry' and rocking Baby Jesus. But the philosophy of the place was simple – you'd either found Jesus, or you hadn't. If you'd found Jesus, you didn't smoke or drink or wear make-up. You didn't go with boys, and you *certainly* didn't go with girls. None of that stuff mattered when you were six, but it sure as hell did when you were sixteen, so most of the kids Kate's age tended to drift away to the Big-Hall churches with youth missions, where they had electric guitars and drums and waved their hands in the air and sang U2 songs on a Sunday. With her mum looking hurt at the very mention of any such defection, that had never been an option for Kate. So, there she was, looking up from filling the tea urn to see her mother gesticulating from her piano stool like a bookie at Ascot, and she knew that it was her Christian duty to go over and greet the new arrivals in a way that would make them want to make the 'Church of the Road' their permanent spiritual home.

At first sight, Susan was an unprepossessing kid. She was chubby, with thin, blonde hair that she was 'growing', pulled back into a tight little ponytail secured by a rubber band. She had the usual adolescent pimples and big, slightly crossed front teeth, but she had bright blue eyes and a cheeky smile, and she looked nice. Susan didn't resemble her mother and sister in the slightest. They were both skinny red-heads and almost carbon copies of each other.

'I don't look anything like my Dad either,' she used to say. 'He always said I must have been the milkman's.'

Kate was never sure whether she was joking about that or not. She'd led a sheltered life.

But on that day they'd only had the chance to exchange names - Susan, Clare and 'Mum', (Mrs Druett) - before Kate's mother launched into the triumphal intro to 'How Great Thou Art' and they all had to shuffle onto the end of the back row of stackable plastic chairs and join in.

'Well, *that* was bloody rousing!' said Susan drily as the final 'aaaaart...' faded away and everyone sat down with a clatter of walking sticks and nose blowing at the sheer emotion of it all.

Kate laughed, despite knowing that she shouldn't. And so, their friendship was forged.

That summer, the two girls became inseparable, and Kate's mum, unusually, encouraged the friendship. She explained quietly to Kate that Mr Druett, Susan's father, had been 'taken into glory' the previous Christmas after a long and painful struggle with cancer. She said that Susan might be appearing to put a good face on things, but had actually taken it very badly. Kate secretly wondered how it would be possible to take it any other way. She noticed that Susan talked about her father as if he were still alive – just temporarily away somewhere, like anyone's dad might be – at work, or at a football match, or down the pub. She wasn't in denial as such. She acknowledged the loss of him when Kate told her how sorry she was. But she liked to keep his memory alive, so she talked about him a lot, and hated the way her mother and sister wouldn't mention him for fear of getting upset.

Mainly though, they just had fun. They rode into town on the bus, took Clare to the park, and had a day out in Southend, with giggles over boys they pretended to fancy, and chips and ice cream for tea before coming back on the train. In between, they spent hours just talking – in the shopping mall, on walks, in each other's bedrooms, and at church where they were supposed to be helping with the summer playgroup.

When they weren't talking, they listened to music, side by side on Susan's bed, with their eyes closed, or bouncing actually *on* the bed, pretending to play air guitars. Susan had inherited a love of rock music from her father. She'd also inherited his record collection, which she added to whenever she could, spending hours in HMV on the High Street, just looking through the CDs and choosing which she would buy when she'd saved up enough from her Christmas and Birthday and doing-the-ironing-for-her-mum money. For Kate, who had been raised on Cliff Richard and Graham Kendrick, the sound of Led Zeppelin, Wishbone Ash, Deep Purple and so many swirling, sinister, hypnotic others, was utterly visceral... a deeply thrilling, but guilty pleasure to be kept secret from her mother and Pastor Eli, who never tired of denouncing 'the devil's music' from his pulpit.

It was the happiest summer of Kate's life.

And then, they went back to school and everything changed.

At lunchtime, Rachel and her two goons were waiting by the tuck shop.

'Hey Ferret... how're you doing? Got any cash on ya'?... Is this yer new girlfriend then?... Su-mo is it then? Or Su-ett? Lick ya' off does she?.... Or dun't she know yer a lezzie?'

As usual, it was Sally and Julie doing the catcalling. Rachel stood slightly behind them, her wavy hair tumbling over the shoulders of her maroon school blazer, looking, for all the world, like a tarty but basically harmless Sixth Former from St Trinians.

'Who the fuck are *they*?' asked Susan, loudly enough for them all to hear.

The two thugs bridled. Behind them, strangely, Rachel smirked. It was almost as if she enjoyed seeing them humiliated.

'**Clearly**, you don't know who runs this place,' said Julie, stepping towards Susan and towering over her.

Susan looked up at her chin. 'Thought it was the headmaster,' she said.

'Yeah.... *right*!...' Julie lurched and Susan sidestepped. For a chubby girl, she was very light on her feet.

Julie wasn't used to people who ducked. She was used to them staying rooted to the spot in terror. So Susan took her by surprise. She staggered on under the force of her own momentum and plopped into the hedge at the side of the shop with her knickers on show to the world.

Several of their schoolmates stopped to snigger.

Kate held her breath and prayed.

Then something very strange happened. The corners of Rachel's mouth lifted. And she laughed out loud. 'Nice one,' she said. 'We're having a girl's night at my place on Saturday. The lads have got an away match, so we thought we'd have fun without them. Seven o'clock. Why don't you come? Bring a bottle.'

Then she turned tail and walked away, leaving Sally to hoist Julie unceremoniously out of the hedge and pick twigs off her blazer.

Susan was not particularly impressed by Rachel and her gang. 'Are you sure you want to go?' she asked when Saturday night came round. 'I reckon we could have a much nicer time just the two of us at the flicks.'

The official story was that they were going to the cinema anyway. They could have gone there easily instead of detouring to Rachel's via Oddbins.

'It's best to keep on the right side of them,' said Kate. Secretly, she was thrilled that Rachel had bestowed this invitation, and she had been on tenterhooks all week, sure that it was all just some sick joke and would be snatched away from them at the eleventh hour.

But Rachel was true to her word. She greeted them at the door of her parents' huge house with a heavy waft of Opium perfume and air kisses against both cheeks. 'I'll get you a drink,' she said, smiling as she took their bottle of Prosecco, which had been described as "light and fruity" at the shop. They followed her into a gleaming black and white kitchen stacked with Schreiber units, a built in hob and an espresso machine that wouldn't have looked out of place in Starbucks. She poured each of them a glass of wine from a big bottle of screw-top white she had open on the worktop. 'We'll put this to chill for a while,' she said, putting the Prosecco in the fridge.

A faint wave of laughter and Britney Spears drifted from a room down the hallway. Susan raised an eyebrow at the music. Rachel noticed. 'I know.... Julie's got very girlie tastes. It's strange when she's such a big butch thing... You'd think she'd be into Death Metal or something like that, wouldn't you? Probably fancies Britney if the truth be known... but don't tell her I said that... I'm more of a Robbie Williams fan myself. I like the bad boys.'

Kate couldn't believe that Rachel Stiles had just shared a joke with them against one of her best friends. She felt ten feet tall as she carried her drink carefully down the hall. She knew that the alcohol was going to be a challenge. Never having touched the stuff before, she figured she'd be safe sticking to one glass. But she'd have been a whole lot safer talking it through with Susan first.

By nine o'clock, the room was spinning. So was the empty Prosecco bottle, in a game of increasingly risqué 'Truth or Dare'.

Sally and Julie and a couple of girls Rachel had introduced as her cousins Jane and Bea were almost as plastered as Kate, though, apparently, they'd helped themselves to Southern Comfort out of Rachel's mum and step-dad's drinks cupboard before Kate and Susan arrived. Everything seemed hilarious. Britney Spears had been replaced by Westlife, much to Susan's continuing disgust. She'd been drinking sparingly and was realising too late that she should have kept more of an eye on Rachel, who also seemed surprisingly sober, as she kept topping up Kate's glass.

The 'Truth' questions were the usual predictable stuff... 'Who do you fancy?' 'How far have you gone with a boy?' 'Have you ever cheated in an exam?' 'Have you ever stolen anything?'...

Then they swerved into darker territory... 'Would you snog Bea's boyfriend if you could get away with it?'... 'If you saw someone being beaten up in the street would you call for help or pretend you hadn't noticed?'... 'What are the top ten meanest things you've ever done to anyone?'

By then, Kate was too drunk to notice that the horrible things they'd done to her didn't even feature in their 'meanest-things' hit parade. She was much too busy hoping that they wouldn't ask her anything about her non-existent sex life. The 'Dares' were becoming more extreme too... 'Five gulps straight down'.... 'Take your top off'..... Then a challenge from Sally... 'Okay Rach, here's a tough one. I dare you to snog Ferret.' She gave a weasel-eyed glance at Sue as she said it and Susan knew that this was meant to hurt her. But she saw the look of jealousy and raw hatred that sprang immediately into Julie's eyes and she realised in that moment what she had probably half-known all along... that Julie was in love with Rachel. When she saw that look, she knew they were on very dangerous ground indeed. She galvanised herself into action to protect her friend. 'Leave it out,' she protested.

'No...' said Rachel. 'I'm up for that.'

Kate felt herself gripped with terror.

'Uuuurgh!!!' chorused Jane and Beatrice, sounding both shocked and amused. 'Don't you dare, or we'll tell your mum.'

'I don't care,' said Rachel. 'I saw her with her tongue down *your* mum's throat last Christmas.'

The mood had changed ominously. Jane looked like she was going to hit her. 'You're a fucking liar!' she said.

'Only joking!' Rachel laughed and the tension seemed to dissipate, though Susan wondered if this was, in fact, true. She never knew what to believe with Rachel. She also wondered how the hell she was going to get Kate home. She wished, not for the first time, that they'd never set foot in this place. 'Look,' she said. 'I think me and Kate need to be going now.'

Rachel exchanged a look with her friends. 'Okay,' she shrugged. 'It was nice of you to come.'

Susan heard sniggers the moment they had left the room. But she guessed that Julie wasn't laughing.

It was a challenge to get Kate past her mother.

'Period pains!' said Susan, knowing that would get *Mr* Ferrings out of the way at least. 'They came on really suddenly at the pictures. Think best thing is straight to bed with a couple of paracetamol and a hot water bottle.' She supported Kate up the narrow staircase, nearly falling down several times on the way up. Kate giggled as they staggered in a heap onto the bed.

'Ssssh!' said Sue.

'Sssssshhhhh....' echoed Kate, giggling again and lifting her finger unsteadily to her lips.

Her mother appeared with the hot water bottle and pain killers.

'Have you two been drinking?' she asked, looking at them suspiciously.

'No, Mrs Ferrings, honest!'

'Well, I'd take a very dim view of it if you had.'

'Absolutely! Me too..... Demon drink, eh?'

'Well, call me if you need me. We're just in the middle of a lovely Doris Day video. Mr Ferrings will drive you home once you've got her settled. We don't want your mum worrying.'

'Thank you Mrs Ferrings.'

Kate spluttered into laughter the minute the door closed, and Susan, frustrated, joined in. 'You'll be getting me into trouble with your wild ways,' she said, fondly. 'Seriously though.... You really *are* a bit of a lezzer, aren't you?'

'No!'

'Yes you *are*! You don't have to pretend with me. It's okay. I don't mind.... But you need to be careful with Rachel....' she stopped, realising that Kate was sliding into sleep. She tucked the hot water bottle against her stomach. 'Whatever you do, *don't* be sick,' she said. 'And I'd save the tablets for tomorrow morning if I were you. You'll need 'em more then.'

'You're the bestest friend in the whole wide world' slurred Kate whoozily.

'Yeah yeah,' said Susan. 'I bet you say that to *all* the girls.'

And so, the weeks went by.

Kate and Sue appeared to be in with Rachel's gang and Kate had a taste of what it was like to be treated with respect by her classmates. Susan kept her reservations to herself as she watched her friend becoming more and more besotted with Rachel.

Then it was the weekend of the Church of the Road's annual prayer retreat in Bognor Regis. Normally Kate would stay with her Auntie Mavis while her parents attended the retreat, but this year, her mother agreed to Susan staying for the weekend instead.

'And remember – no parties!' she said, sternly, as Kate's dad loaded their suitcases into the car.

'No Mum, I promise.'

'And no boys.'

'No – definitely not.'

'Stew's in the fridge.... and trifle for afters.'

'Thanks Mum.'

'And you've got the number of the centre if there are any problems.'

'Yep... Go on Mum... We'll be fine... You two just forget about me and have a lovely relaxing weekend.'

She felt a jolt of sadness as she waved goodbye to her parents. She could see that her mum was eagerly looking forward to two days of worship songs and stimulating talks while her dad was just looking forward to Monday when he could get back to work and into his old familiar routine.

She made herself a cup of tea and settled down to do her homework. Susan was due late afternoon. It was going to be good fun.

At four o'clock, the doorbell rang. This was unusual. Sue normally just knocked and came straight in.

Kate went to see who was at the door.

It was Rachel. 'Hey,' she said. 'How're you doing?'

Kate's heart did a little somersault. 'I'm fine. I was expecting Sue.' She looked down the road to see if she could see any sign of her friend.

'Yeah... that's why I'm here. I just bumped into her. She was coming to tell you, her mum's got a migraine and she's having to stay home and make tea for Clare.'

'Oh!' Kate felt a twinge of disappointment, then fear, as she wondered if she was facing the prospect of a night in the house on her own. 'She's coming later though, right?'

'She said she'd come round tomorrow.'

'Oh... right,' Kate tried to look cool about it and knew she failed. 'I'll give her a ring later, see how her mum is.'

'Nah... that's why she didn't call herself. Their phone's out of order.'

'Oh... right!' Waves of dejection washed over Kate. She felt tears stinging at the back of her eyes.

'Hey, fancy some company for a while?' Rachel looked kind, concerned.

Kate felt grateful instantly. 'Yes,' she said. 'That would be lovely.'

It was wonderful being alone with Rachel, basking in the glow of her attention, listening to her talking about her life, her difficult relationship with her step-dad, her doubts about whether Mike was actually 'the one' or not. She seemed interested in Kate too. She wanted to know all about Church.... What it was like to be a Christian....

How she'd met Susan... Did she bear any resentment about all the times they'd 'teased' her?

About six o'clock, Rachel said, 'Hey, I've had an idea... How about I phone my mum and ask if I can stay the night. I'm sure she'd say yes.'

Kate felt like a whole flock of butterflies had taken off in her stomach. 'That would be great,' she said. 'But, are you sure you haven't got other stuff you'd rather be doing?

Rachel smiled into her eyes. 'I'd rather be here,' she said. 'With you.'

Somehow, after they'd eaten, they ended up on the sofa and Rachel mentioned the game of Truth or Dare.

'I keep thinking about it,' she said. 'What would have happened if Sue hadn't insisted on you going home.'

'Me too!'

'She was jealous you know.'

'Don't be daft.'

'She was... she's just *so* into you.'

'I don't think so.'

'Well... whatever... she rescued you. I know you wouldn't have actually *wanted* to kiss me.' Rachel looked shy suddenly.

Kate, felt breathless, as if her throat was closing. She felt blood pulsing in her neck... a blush spreading slowly from her chest.... creeping up into her cheeks. 'I wouldn't actually say that,' she stammered.

'Oh?' Rachel raised an eyebrow, tilted her head and looked at her sideways. 'Don't tell me that Julie and Sally are right about you then?'

Kate felt frightened then. 'No... no... of course not.'

'Well, which is it then? You'd *like* to kiss me... or you wouldn't?'

She'd moved closer. Her lips were so close to Kate's she could feel the warmth of her breath on her face.

'I...'

Rachel leaned in just slightly as she started to speak... brushing her lips against Kate's.

'You...?'

'I don't know....'

Rachel smiled and kissed her, running the tip of her tongue softly against Kate's lips. 'Maybe it's time you *did* know.... Maybe I could teach you...'

It felt wrong to be kissing there, on that red moquette sofa where her mum did her knitting and watched fifties movies on video. Where she'd sat on her dad's knee and had stories read to her as a child. Where her mum had cried when she heard the news of her own mother's death and Kate had tried to comfort her and failed. But she did it anyway, too excited by Rachel's tongue gently teasing its way between her lips, Rachel's hand cupping itself over her breast, feeling the exquisite pressure of that hand, squeezing gently through the thin material of her T-shirt and bra.

From the sideboard, her mum and dad's wedding photograph reproved her.

She couldn't bear it.

'Would you like to go upstairs?' she asked, shakily.

Rachel grinned. 'Thought you'd never ask,' she said. And there was something about the way she said it that made Kate feel very scared indeed.

She assumed it was normal to be frightened.

And so she leant against her bedroom door and heard it clicking shut behind her as Rachel pinned her there, cupping her face with both hands, running her fingers through her hair, kissing her urgently, all over her face. 'Touch me,' she said, unbuttoning her shirt and guiding Kate's hands inside.

Kate heard the soft, barely perceptible catch in her breathing as she ran her fingers over the rough black lace bra. 'You *really* want me, don't you?' Rachel whispered the words into Kate's mouth, biting very gently on her lip, reaching behind herself and struggling for just a moment with the bra clasp. Then Kate felt the soft, delicious weight of her breasts as they sank into her hands. And her own body kicked in response, hot and wet, betraying her.

'Here...' Rachel's breathing was ragged as she pulled Kate back onto the bed, unbuttoning her jeans, unzipping them quickly and arching her back to ease them down over her hips. She took Kate's hand again...

They leapt apart guiltily as the doorbell rang. For a second, Rachel looked confused. She glanced at the clock, irritated. Then she composed herself.

'Oh, that'll be Mike,' she said casually, smoothing her clothes as she stood up. 'He's always bloody early. Can't wait to see me I suppose. Shame though, I was quite enjoying that! Maybe we can do it again sometime.... Or maybe not, eh?' She straightened her hair. 'Oh well... I'd better go and let him in. Don't bother coming down. We'll probably just go straight to bed anyway.'

It was a sleepless night as Kate lay, trying to block out the sounds from her parents' room next door. She was ashamed and humiliated, fighting back tears that came anyway. She wished she could talk to Sue. But she knew that she would never be able to tell her about this. She knew, in fact, that she would never be able to tell *anyone* about how utterly degraded she felt that night.

It was hard to know how the night finally lightened into dawn and the time ticked away past eight, nine, ten, eleven... when Rachel and Mike finally emerged barely dressed from the room. They had a strange musky smell about them. Kate wondered how she would ever air her parents' room before they got home. 'Any chance of a cup of tea,' asked Mike, rubbing at his tousled head as he yawned until his jaw cracked. 'It really *was* good of you to let me come round like this Katie. I know there'd be hell to pay if your mum and dad ever found out.'

Kate averted her eyes from his Metallica T-shirt and boxer shorts and went to put the kettle on.

'Is there any hot water for a bath?' asked Rachel. 'Better not go home smelling like a slag.'

'Yes, the immersion heater's on timer.' How Kate hated her now she knew what she was capable of. She kept her eyes on the floor. It felt safer. 'Would *you* like some tea?'

'Yeah... some toast would be nice too... if you're making some.'

Kate knew it was an order. She put bread onto the grill.

Somehow she tolerated them laughing and feeding each other toast at the kitchen table. She watched as they ate half a jar of marmalade between them, giving each other buttery kisses between mouthfuls. She knew that Mike was oblivious to her distress, smiling at her, teasing her a bit, trying to include her in the conversation, assuming that her quietness was just because she was shy.

He hugged her when they were finally on their way out.

Rachel hung back in the hallway. Her lips were still greasy from the toast. 'By the way,' she said. 'Do you remember when we locked you in the cellar for a couple of hours to get your dinner money out of you?'

Kate nodded, shuddering as she remembered. For a moment she thought that Rachel was going to apologise. But she was wrong. 'We left your girlfriend in there overnight,' she said. 'She might be a bit cold now. I'd go and let her out if I were you.'

Kate ran until the breath tore at her chest and her heart felt like it would burst. She panted over the railway bridge where the Intercity Express screamed beneath her... past the bus stop... the medical centre... the park. It was a cold morning and it had been a colder night. The sky was grey, spitting rain. She ran with tears stinging her cheeks and dribbling into the corners of her mouth where she tasted them salty, having to stop to blow her nose and fight the cramp that had stitched itself into her side. And as she ran she was praying to a God she barely believed in anymore for Susan to be alright... for her not to even *be* in that awful place... for this to be just another of Rachel's sick jokes.

The house was set apart from the rest of the fairly substantial dwellings on a tree-lined avenue about five minutes walk from the school. Its heavily overgrown gardens had once been lovingly planned and cared for. Kate had never ventured near it since the day they imprisoned her there, five years ago. It was much more dilapidated now. But she remembered the way in, through the gap in the hedge, where the junkies and the prostitutes came and went. Now its windows were smashed, walls graffitied, boards ripped off the front door, which swung open onto a hallway that stank of urine and mould. It was hard to believe that anyone could ever have been happy there. Kate heard scuffling in one of the rooms to her right. She didn't know whether it was an animal or a person or just something blowing around in the draught from the broken window. It flashed through her mind that this might be a trap. That Sally and Julie might be waiting there in the shadows for her. But she pushed on, creeping along the hallway to the kitchen. She remembered the rubbish on the worktops, the burnt spoons that had been used for shooting up. She remembered the syringes on the floor too, and how they'd threatened to stab her with one of those. She saw immediately how they'd pulled the fridge freezer across in front of the cellar door. It explained the eerie scraping noise she'd heard when they shut her in.... and again when they came to let her out. She wanted to call out to Sue. To tell her she was there and it was going to be okay. But she was afraid to draw attention to herself. So she squeezed herself between the side of the fridge and the wall and half lifted, half pushed it, inch by painful inch until it was clear of the door and she could open it to reveal the blackness beyond. For a moment, there was only silence. Then her eyes adjusted to the gloom and she saw the figure huddled on the stairs, terrified eyes trying to make out the identity of the person silhouetted in the doorway, against the light. The voice was barely recognisable as Sue's. 'I'm sorry. I won't do it again,' she begged. 'Please let me go now.'

'Oh God!' Kate daren't venture through the door. She knelt and held out her hand. 'I'm so sorry,' she whispered. 'Come on, we've got to get out of here.'

Later, when they were safely home, Sue finally allowed herself to cry – huge, juddering dry sobs that felt like they were being ripped out of the very guts of her. She gripped Kate's sweatshirt, burying her face into her shoulder, shaking uncontrollably with the force of her terror.

'How did you find me?' she asked at last.

Kate should have been prepared for this, but she wasn't. 'Rachel told me,' she said. 'I ran all the way.'

'Why didn't you look for me when I didn't turn up?'

Kate heard the mild accusation in Sue's voice. She felt what Sue must have felt.... the sense of utter abandonment... knowing that if she screamed she might bring even worse upon herself.... She imagined what it must have been like not wanting even those monsters to leave her there in that God-forsaken place alone.

'Rachel said your mum was poorly. And she said your phone wasn't working.'

'Oh,' said Susan. 'You always *were* a fool for Rachel.'

'Do you want the lowdown on the online chatter then?' Jaiden was remarkably upbeat for someone who had just spent half the night lurking in the troll infested swamps of social media-land.

Saskia glanced at her out of the corner of a jaded eye. Despite the vodka, and the apparent roominess of her brother's bed, she had found herself incapable of sleeping next to Naz and had crept out in the early hours to lie on the sofa and watch the city slowly waking in a haze of pink and lilac.

Jaiden took her lack of response as encouragement. 'Everybody pretty much hated Rachel,' she went on. 'No surprise there. Well, apart from the husband and the friend who owns the bar, that is.... *They're* both devastated. But there are a lot of people who're really glad to see the back of her and perfectly happy to go public with their opinions. Some pretty sick jokes too, if I'm honest. But the bad news is that everybody thinks Kate did it. They think she finally snapped and "bagged the bitch", as Sally Ballantree put it.'

'The Sally we are visiting now?' Saskia may have been only half listening, but she recognised the name.

'Yeah, the one who used to be in Rachel's gang... Interesting, eh?'

'Mm,' Saskia nodded. She was troubled by the memory of Naz, breathing softly under the thin T-shirt she wore in bed. Remembering the way her hair curled, ink-black against the white of the pillowcase, her fist clutching the top of the continental quilt, tucked up under her chin, her long, dark lashes flickering against the top of her cheekbones as she dreamt – probably of Kate, Saskia told herself as a kind of punishment.

She was so angry with Mik for putting his damned suspicions into her mind. Until he'd voiced them, she felt sure her feelings for Naz had been pure. But now the thought he'd planted had continued to grow. And she knew that she loved her friend, impossibly and too late. The idea was all the harder because she knew that she might, at some point have had a chance of developing a relationship with Naz, but had, instead, blindly, stupidly, pushed her in Kate's direction, not knowing for one minute then, how much she would regret it now.

'Wonder what happened?' she said, as if she'd been thinking of Sally and her rift with Rachel all along.

'Yeah,' said Jaiden. 'People are fascinating aren't they..? That's one of the reasons I love my job so much.'

Sally was still in her dressing gown when she opened the door. It was navy blue, knee-length and velour, and may once have fitted her. 'Can't offer you a cup of tea,' she said, as she led them into the untidy sitting room, past a kitchen piled with rancid pots and pans. 'Milk's off.'

That's a blessing thought Jaiden. 'No worries,' she said. 'I know you must be very busy and we're just very grateful to you for seeing us. We won't keep you long, I promise.'

Sally shrugged. She didn't look like someone who needed to be anywhere in a hurry. She moved a pile of 'Closer' magazines and a damp towel to make room on the sofa for them to sit down. 'My mum passes 'em on to me when she's read 'em,' she said, as if she needed to explain herself. 'But I don't just sit around on me arse all day reading magazines you know. It's not easy when you're on your own with a kid.'

'I'm sure it isn't,' said Jaiden soothingly.

'Especially a boy. They don't help like a girl would.'

'Is hard,' said Saskia, sympathetically.

Sally fixed her with a sharp look. 'Where'd *you* come from then?' she asked.

'Slovakia.'

'Huh!' Sally tutted.

Jaiden thought she'd better change the subject before they were treated to the gospel according to Nigel Farage. 'We're on Kate Ferrings' legal team,' she said.

Sally gave a mirthless snort. 'Well, good luck with that!'

To Saskia's surprise, Jaiden laughed with her. 'We're certainly having an uphill struggle,' she said. 'But we're hopeful that we can get Kate home soon.'

Sally snorted again. 'Why... d'ya think they'll let her off for services to humanity?' She crossed her legs for emphasis, revealing pallid and very dimpled thighs under the dressing gown.

Jaiden leaned forward casually. Saskia noticed that she kept her eyes resolutely away from Sally's thigh region. She tried to do the same, but she found she kept getting drawn back there. It was like trying to pass an accident on the motorway without rubber-necking.

'I'm surprised to hear you say that,' said Jaiden, sounding scarily honest as she lied. 'I thought you were a *friend* of Rachel's.'

'Not anymore.' She folded her arms. 'Hah... well obviously... not anymore, eh? Not now she's dead. But even before that... not since the cow nicked my bloke.'

'But I thought she was married.'

'Open all hours,' said Sally. Then when both Jaiden and Saskia looked blank... 'They were swingers... Well... Rachel mainly... Mike usually ended up sat there playing 'Candy Crush' on his smart phone, if you get my drift.'

Saskia was not at all sure that she did.

But Jaiden seemed to be keeping up, at least. 'So how come she nicked your bloke? Isn't that against the rules.'

'Against all rules of decent behaviour, yes... the cow.'

'How long had you and....'

'Jed... Jed Watkins.'

'How long had you and Jed been together?'

'Six months.'

'How did you meet him? It can't be easy.... With a kid, I mean.'

'No, it isn't. I met him on-line.'

'And it was a serious relationship?'

'Yeah. Very.'

'So, when did Rachel meet him?'

'He used to come into work to see me. I'd slip him an odd free drink, you know, when no-one was looking. He's on benefits, so he doesn't have a lot of spare cash.... Anyway, Rach had come in to see Julie...'

'Sorry... you're losing me...'

'Oh, yeah... I was working at Julie's place...'

'Pulsations?'

'Yeah... yeah.... And anyway, on this day Rachel came in and I could see straight away that she fancied him, the bitch. Next thing I know, she's leaving bloody Mike for him.'

Jaiden and Saskia both tutted and nodded sympathetically.

'Is love rat!' said Saskia fiercely.

Sally looked at her as if she'd gone mad. 'Not *him*,' she said. 'Dunno, maybe you do it different in Croatia.'

'Slovakia.'

'Whatever... But he's just a bloke. Can't help his self... No, it's her... Nicking a mate's fella. That's totally not okay. It was the one thing we said we'd never do.'

'I can see why you're angry,' said Jaiden encouragingly.

'Angry don't even *begin* to express it, mate.'

'Do you still work at Pulsations?' asked Jaiden.

'No way!' Sally scoffed and lit a cigarette. 'Not once that bloody tart got involved there.'

'How was she involved?'

'She was going into the business with Julie. Frigging cows, the pair of 'em. No bloody loyalty anywhere in the world no more.'

'Are you sure about that? Rachel was definitely going into business with Julie?'

'Yeah... bar was going down the nick. Just between you and me, there'd been some dealing going on... nothing serious... bit of Charlie... bit of weed... and we'd been raided a couple of times. A lot of the regulars got scared off and it needed a re-launch. Rach had all sorts of big ideas for the place. She was planning on sinking her divorce settlement into it. Bet Julie's gutted about Ferret toppin' her before she got her hands on the money. Bloody serves her right if you ask me.'

'Kate says that you and Julie and Rachel used to bully her. Is that true?'

Sally shook her head shiftily. 'Nah... bit of teasing that's all. She was such a freaky little weirdo and then she had that great lump of a mate in tow. Looked like Little and bleedin' Large. Total freaks.... Massive crush on Rach too.... Bet she didn't tell you that, uh?'

'Well, as it happens, she did. Have the police interviewed you?'

'Yeah... Came a couple of days ago. Jude... something or other.'

'Jules Mullen?'

'That's the one.... She had some bloke with her, don't remember his name.'

'Have you actually got an alibi for the day Rachel was killed?'

Surprisingly Sally didn't appear to be offended by this. 'Hah... you mean might I have done it? I'd love to have, I'll tell ya. But no, I had more important things to do. I was in a clinic, getting rid of Jed's baby as it happens. Bloody ironic, eh?'

'Oh, God, I'm sorry!'

'Not half as sorry as me, mate. I thought he was the one.'

Jaiden fell silent, thinking. Suddenly she looked up. 'This might sound like a daft question,' she said. 'But is there anyone at Pulsations who looks anything like Rachel... You know, blonde, long wavy hair, thirtyish. Anybody who could be mistaken for her at a distance?'

Sally stubbed out her cigarette as she pondered. 'Maybe Mandy,' she said. 'Why?'

Jaiden ignored the question. 'Do you know her surname?' she asked.

'Simmons, I think.... But why?'

'Just trying to introduce a shadow of a doubt,' said Jaiden.

'Oh... right... to get Ferret off?'

'Something like that.'

'Well,' she shrugged. 'I won't argue with that. Mandy could easy be mistaken for Rachel at a distance. If there's anything more I can help with, you let me know. But don't tell Julie I told you. She's a total bleedin' psycho *that* one. I might not be friends with her no more, but I sure as hell don't want to get on the wrong side of her.'

'Well, *that* was a game-changer!' Jaiden whistled appreciatively as they headed down the concrete stairs from Sally Ballantree's flat.

'But what if she warns Julie?' Saskia was naturally paranoid. It was a quality that had always served her well.

'If she warns her, we've got problems. That's why I've blu-tacked a nice bit of audio-surveillance kit under her coffee table. It'll phone me the minute anybody talks.'

'Is that legal?'

'God no... but she's hardly likely to find it, is she? That place hasn't seen housework in years.... Think we need to get a picture of Mandy to Kate next. How do you fancy going undercover with me at Pulsations?'

Susan's houseboat had a permanent mooring on the Thames not far from Richmond Bridge. Since Saskia had been commandeered to taxi Jaiden to visit Sally and Julie, Naz was on public transport. She'd taken the tube across to Richmond and then walked through the town, over the bridge and down a rather unpromising dirt track, following the battered London A to Z that David had lent to her. Now she opened a creaky wooden gate with a letterbox on a pole beside it, and wondered whether to take the path straight ahead to the boat, or the short fork to the large log cabin on the bank.

She tried the boat first, standing ankle deep in grass and calling 'Hello?' over the splash of the water and squawking of the river birds, until the answering silence on board led her back up the slight incline towards the cabin.

At least there was a door to knock on there, but the silence from within was just as intense as before. *'Damn it!'* sighed Naz. This was exactly what she'd feared, since she was arriving unannounced. But she'd psyched herself up for meeting Susan... running through the questions Jaiden had told her to ask all the way there. And now she was hot, wound up, and disappointed.

She was rummaging in her bag for a pen to write a note when the gate creaked behind her and a voice asked 'Can I help you?'

She swung round to see a chubby and heavily sweating blonde struggling through the gate with two bulging Bags-for-Life in each hand. She looked at Naz warily.

'Are you Susan Druett?'

'Yes....' Her face took on a 'and *you* are?' kind of look. She looked as if she might make a run for it if Naz gave the wrong answer.

'I'm Naz... I'm a friend of Kate Ferrings'...'

'Kate?.... Is she okay?' Something in Naz's tone must have conveyed that she wasn't.

'You've not heard then?'

'No.... tell me, you're frightening me now. What's happened?' She put the bags down on the grass and glared into Naz's face.

Naz told her, as carefully and gently as she could, but there was no easy way to say it. She felt bad as she saw the shock on Susan's face.

'I thought you might have seen it in the papers,' she said. She'd hoped so, at least.

'No... I never read them. They're too depressing... Shit... poor Kate... Can I see her?'

'Not while the police are questioning her, but if you give me your phone number I can let you know as soon as there's any news. In the meantime, I wondered if I could talk to you? I mean, it goes without saying that she couldn't have done it. And we wondered if you might have any ideas about who might have wanted to set her up like this.'

'Who's "we"?' This woman really *was* wary.

'Her lawyer... and... and her friends, I guess.'

Sue rubbed her eyes and pushed her hair back from her hot cheeks. 'God yes, of course. We can talk in the cabin...' She unlocked the door. 'I'll just take this stuff onto the boat. Don't want everything defrosting all over the place. I won't be long. Just make yourself at home.'

Naz looked around the cabin while she was gone. It was hot from being locked up in the sunshine and it smelt of wood. There was a very old looking orange and brown rug on the floor, and a log burning stove for winter. A sofa that also looked like it had seen better days, swathed in a brown throw and piled high with cushions, faced an unbleached cotton Ikea chair. There was a sink unit with a small fridge. And a desk, untidy with books and papers, was stationed in front of the window, with a view across the river to Richmond on the far bank.

Naz moved some of the cushions out of the way and sat uncertainly on the sofa. It 'gave' rather more than it should have done under her slightness.

'Can I get you a drink?' asked Sue as she returned from her unpacking.

'Oh, yes please. I'm quite thirsty.'

'Me too... spitting bloody feathers actually! What would you like? I've got some lager, coffee, tea... water in the tap.'

'A cup of tea would be nice.'

'No probs.... I think I might have some biscuits too somewhere in here... ah yes...' She rooted around in a filing cabinet by the desk, producing a small pile of Penguins, Fruit Clubs, and a packet of Peanut Cookies. Naz accepted a Penguin, wondering if they'd got smaller or she'd got bigger since she had one last.

'D'ya take sugar?' asked Sue.

'No thank you, just milk.'

Susan handed her a mug and her business card. 'While I'm thinking about it,' she said. 'Don't want you leaving without my number.'

Naz read the card. 'Computer Aided Design? Sounds technical.'

'Yeah, it's interesting, it pays well and I can do it from home. I'm not always all that keen on going out.' She sat down in the Ikea chair. 'I'm still reeling,' she said. 'Rachel Stiles, dead... Bloody hell! And poor Kate, she must be in bits....' Naz noticed that she was shaking slightly. 'And you're a friend of Kate's. How come I haven't heard of you? Are you one of her therapy buddies then?'

'No,' Naz hesitated. She was actually quite uncertain of her status in Kate's life right now. She also wasn't sure how 'out' Kate was with her friends.

Sue looked at her with her head on one side. Then she made it easy for her. 'Good God!' she said suddenly. 'You're not actually a *girlfriend* are you?'

Naz nodded and sipped at her tea to hide her embarrassment.

'Shit, after all these years... I can't believe it..... She always *did* go for the pretty girls. Tried her best not to care about stuff like that, but she does. It's that perfectionist streak I reckon. So, how long have *you* been on the scene then?'

'Not long.' Naz found herself blushing.

'Well how bloody typical of Kate. She never *did* have any luck, but this takes the biscuit.... Finally gets round to finding herself a bird and gets banged up for murder!'

Naz laughed, despite herself. 'Yeah... I think I've put a jinx on her. She'd known me less than 24 hours before we ended up stuck in a lift together.'

'She won't have liked *that* much!' Sue raised an eyebrow and took a shaky sip of her tea. 'She'll like a police cell even less though, I can tell you... She can't *stand* being locked in... And for Rachel fucking Stiles too... I can't believe it.'

For a moment, Naz was distracted. 'How come she's so phobic?' she asked.

Sue hesitated... 'She got locked in somewhere when she was a kid. But she doesn't really talk about it.... You know how she is, all buttoned up...'

'Yeah. People don't get it. They think she's just a pain in the neck. But she's not like that at all really.'

'Well, it's a bad combination – driven and shy. You've just got to make sure you tell her to get a grip when she gets too far up herself. Otherwise she'll drive you nuts.'

'I'll do my best,' said Naz wryly. 'If we ever get her out of this... and if she still wants me if we do.' When she put it like that, the odds seemed to be stacked so heavily against her. She rushed on to distract herself from the feeling of depression that welled up whenever she thought about it. 'So, *can* you think of anyone who might have a grudge against both of them?'

Sue hunkered back in her chair, holding the mug in both hands to steady it as she took another gulp. 'Not really,' she said. 'They were never exactly batting for "the same team".'

'Rachel and her gang used to bully her... is that right?'

'Yeah – relentlessly.'

'Did they bully you too?'

'Yep.'

'How come?'

'Do bullies *need* a reason?'

Naz was afraid suddenly that she wasn't doing this right; that she wouldn't know what was relevant and what wasn't. She wished that she had Saskia, or David or Jaiden with her to keep her on the right track. 'I guess not,' she said. 'So, there wasn't any particular reason why Rachel had such a downer on Kate?'

Sue took another slurp of her tea and wrinkled her nose. 'God knows what goes on in the minds of people like that. The woman was a sociopath and so were her mates.'

'Yeah, but she targeted Kate all through school. It feels personal to me. You *must* have a theory.'

'Maybe.'

'It might be helpful.'

'Okay... and it *is* just a theory. But I think it was because she fancied her.'

'Kate fancied Rachel?'

Sue laughed bitterly. 'Of course *Kate* fancied Rachel. *Everybody* fancied Rachel. I even fancied her myself until I discovered what a total snake she was. But no.... that wasn't the problem. I always thought the problem was that Rachel fancied Kate. I think she quite admired her too, in a funny sort of a way. And that's why she hated her so much. Didn't fit in with her plans you see. Footballer's wife, loads of dosh, exotic holidays abroad. Fame, fortune and celebrity. She had it all mapped out, and she was never giving that lot up for something as inconvenient as Kate.'

'So, there was some kind of connection between them?'

'If you want to call it that.'

'Do you think it's possible that Rachel *might* have gone to Kate for help?'

'It's possible, I guess. It's the kind of thing she might have done just as a wind up. But Kate wouldn't have seen her. No way!'

'Okay.' Naz tried a different tack. 'Mr Ferrings thinks that something happened to you and Kate when you had a sleepover at their place while they were away on some Church thing.'

Susan blanched. 'God was it *that* obvious?' she said, half to herself.

'He thinks you may have had some boys round, or a party that got out of hand or something.'

'Nah... we were much too well behaved for all that... or Kate was, at any rate.... No, that was actually the weekend that Rachel's gang locked me overnight in the cellar.'

'*Overnight?*'

'Twenty hours to be precise. They certainly surpassed themselves that weekend.'

'But how come no-one came looking for you?'

'I was supposed to be staying with Kate, and Rachel went round there and told her I couldn't come because my mum was ill.'

'And she *believed* her?'

'Yes... and I don't think she's ever forgiven herself for that. But it was complicated. They'd been pretending to be friendly... lulled us into a false sense of security. We should have known really. But I don't think it even crossed Kate's mind to imagine that Rachel might be lying to her. She *was* very good at it, I must say.'

'So, how did you get out?'

'Rachel told Kate on the Sunday morning. Told her where I was. It could have been a lot worse. She might never have told her at all. I thought I was going to die down there.'

'It must have been awful!'

'It's okay. I don't think about it much anymore.' Clearly, this was untrue. Naz saw her shudder. 'I was a bit of a mess at first though. Kate's been on a one-woman mission to 'cure' me ever since. Had me going for therapy - EMDR, TIR, EFT... you name it, I've had it. I don't get the nightmares so much anymore. 'Specially since I've been with Brenda.'

'Your partner?'

'Yeah. I feel safer when she's around. It helps.'

'Look, are you okay to talk about this?'

'Yes, truly, I'm fine.'

'Okay,' Naz took a deep breath. It didn't *feel* fine. She could see that this was raking it all up. 'So... who actually locked you in? Was it Rachel?'

'No, I think Rachel was the mastermind, but she never did any of the physical stuff. She didn't need to. She was in a league of her own. Total head-fucker... No, it was Julie and Sally who grabbed me and shoved me in there. They chucked me down the cellar steps... cracked a couple of ribs.... knackered my wrist. But the worst thing was that they told me the place was haunted. I know it sounds stupid now. I'd have thought it was stupid then in broad daylight. But they told me this awful story. They said that an old couple had lived there and they'd never had any children. The old man had turned part of the cellar into a workshop. And one day, he cut himself so badly he bled to death on the floor there. And his wife was so distraught that she never got over it and ended up committing suicide and rotting upstairs for ages before anybody found her. They said nobody would live there anymore, because the place was haunted and on a night you could hear her walking about and wailing for her husband. It was a load of bollocks of course. I researched it later as part of my therapy. Actually, the old lady died in a nursing home and her husband died in a hospice three years later. The place was falling to bits because a load of distant relatives were fighting over the will. A big detached house like that in London. The land alone is worth a mint. I didn't know that then though. They left me with a tea light candle that ran out after about four hours. No food. No water. And all because Julie thought I'd shown her up when she tripped over her own feet a few weeks before. People who do stuff like that... their egos are so fragile. They can't stand being embarrassed. I should have known not to take them on, but I was cocky back then. Too cocky for my own good, as it happens.'

Naz nodded. She'd learnt that early on at the children's home. The cocky kids were always either integrated or destroyed. She remembered what Jaiden had told them in the pub, about Sue's suicide attempt later. 'I'm guessing you never reported this to anyone?'

She scoffed at the idea. 'Now *that* would have been *really* stupid,' she said.

Naz knew that. Of course she did.

She looked glumly at Susan. 'All this just keeps looking worse and worse for Kate,' she sighed. 'She had so many reasons for wanting Rachel dead.'

'Yes,' said Sue. 'But there's a big difference between wanting someone dead and actually killing them.... How *did* she actually die, by the way?'

'An overdose of tranquillisers and a plastic bag over her head.... Awful, eh?'

Sue jumped. 'That's exactly how the old girl at the house was supposed to have done it!' she said. 'That can't just be co-incidence surely. That place was their punishment block. They must have had other kids in there. I didn't know until afterwards, but they'd done it to Kate when she was eleven. It was only for a couple of hours, but that's a hell of a long time for a kid. And it's what goes on in your head that gets to you...'

'Which is why she can't stand being locked in! God, I wish I'd known that. I'd never have let her get in that stupid lift.'

'Yes, but don't you see... This really opens it up. It could have been anyone that Rachel's gang locked in that cellar.'

For a moment, Naz's heart lifted. Then it came crashing down again. 'But wouldn't it need to be someone with a grudge against Kate too?' she asked.

'I dunno... I need to get my head around this. Kate will have a good idea who the other victims might have been. Tell her solicitor to ask her. And anything I can do to help... anything at all. You just phone me okay?'

She walked Naz to the gate. 'Kate never was the same after that weekend,' she said. 'She felt so guilty.'

Naz nodded. She'd seen that in Kate. It would have been awful for her to know that her friend had suffered like that, especially when she already knew what it felt like. She worried too much about people at the best of times. It was one of the things that made her such a pain in the backside. Like at Horton Hill when she was so bothered that the people at the conference might hate the venue. She'd got agitated on their behalf and then she'd felt guilty about giving the staff a hard time while she was 'off on one'.

'I wish she could be kinder to herself,' she said sadly. 'It doesn't sound like *you* blame her at all. And she got you out of there as soon as she knew what had happened.'

'Yeah... but guilt doesn't work like that, does it? As far as I can see, people who *should* feel guilty never actually feel any guilt at all. They just think it's all everybody else's fault.... "Just look what you made me do..." all that kind of thing... And people like Kate.... well, *she* feels guilty all the bloody time – about everything.'

'Yeah... I guess...' She could see that Sue was hesitating... unsure whether to say something or not. She left space. Sue took it.

'And we never actually talked about it, but I've always thought....'

More space.... Naz nodded slightly, encouraging. She daren't speak for fear of saying the wrong thing.

Finally, Sue finished the sentence. 'I've always thought that Kate slept with Rachel that night,' she said. And it was a relief to voice the suspicion that had lived with her, unspoken, for fourteen years.

Naz stopped by the bridge and looked out over the river. She wondered how to condense what she had just discovered. Above her the sky was blue, dotted with high white clouds. People walked by laughing, enjoying the sunshine. Across the street, a crowd of students were sitting outside a bar, drinking. All around it was just a normal Saturday.

Then a car radio blasted 'Stay with Me,' into the warm weekend air, and she noticed that her hand was shaking as she took out her phone.

Beneath her, the water that had lapped gently against Sue's home just moments before continued its long grey journey to the sea.

Saskia felt good slipping back into her 'Saskia Prochazka' persona. Even re-adopting the accent, she felt a sense of freedom she never possessed when she was 'just' being herself. She wondered, as she walked into Pulsations, if she might actually prefer to be 'Saskia Prochazka' all the time.

'Good God, a customer!' said the handsome young man behind the bar.

Generally guys like that were only prepared to be with her when they'd had several pints of Stella, but she was starting to realise that they showed her a lot more attention when she was in 'Prochazka mode'. While she was at Horton Hill, she'd just assumed that Yorkshire men liked their girls more sturdy, but this guy wasn't a Northerner and he was clearly interested. He was also gorgeous. She noticed that his T-shirt was tight, emphasising a torso that Bradley, who oversaw the remnants of the leisure centre at Horton Hill, would refer to as 'ripped'. In the old days, she would have told herself that she fancied him. Now, she felt strangely indifferent to his charms.

Since he'd got so excited though, she thought she'd better buy a drink. 'Coke with ice please,' she said, hitching herself with some difficulty onto the barstool. 'And whatever you would like for yourself.'

She looked around her at the stained wooden floor with lights studded into it, black toughened glass tables and shabby black seats. The video of 'Blurred Lines' was playing on a large, flat screen TV mounted over the bar. The place had a stale, beery smell, like her father when she was a child.

'Tchah!!' she tutted, watching the video. 'Was told this place was "classy".'

The barman laughed. 'Only if you've got *very* low standards.... I'm Martin, by the way.'

'Good morning Martin. Is good to meet.... Cheers!' She raised her glass to him, noticing that he'd put the money for his drink straight into the tight back pocket of his jeans.

'Cheers!' he said.

'Will come straight to point,' said Saskia. 'And please take eyes from my cleavage.'

'Oh sorry... didn't realise I was...'

'Is okay.... I come for job.'

Martin looked puzzled. 'I don't think we've advertised anything,' he said.

'No... not advertised... I talk with one of girls... blonde... Mandy...'

'Oh, yeah... Mandy...'

'She think I find work here. Shit hot on bar. Perfect shake-off cocktail.... Sex on Beach... Talking Monkey.... Screwdriver... All in here...' She pointed to her head.

'Yeah... I'm sure... but thing is...'

'More tradition?... Mojito.... Bellini.... Daiquiri... All here.'

'Yeah, but thing is, Mandy was probably talking to you when we still thought we were going to be expanding.'

'Yes, is right... expanding!'

'No, I'm sorry. Our backer went and got herself killed.'

'Noooo? Is dreadful!'

'Yeah. Reckon I'll be down the job centre myself next week.'

'Aacchh!!!'

'Yeah... It's bad.'

'Is shit-luck!'

He looked like he might giggle at this, but he managed to keep a straight face. 'Yes, you're right. It *is* shit-luck.'

Saskia sipped moodily at her Coke, feeling like Greta Garbo - double whiskey, ginger ale on the side.... 'When she come in?' she asked eventually.

'Who...?'

'Mandy!... Who else I talk about... Should see.... Say hello.... then goodbye.' She took a deep gulp of her drink and swung her legs innocently.

'She should be in this lunchtime,' he said. 'She usually starts about half eleven, though at this rate, the boss'll be sending us both home again before two. You could try talking to *her* if you want. Though I think she'll just tell you exactly the same as I've told you. *She* should be in by twelve. You're welcome to wait you know.' He looked as if he would have liked her to. She figured he must get lonely there behind his bar, all by himself.

'No,' she abandoned the Coke. 'Shop first. Back later.'

'Okay,' he called after her. 'See you later then. Hey, what's your name, by the way?'

She may have answered his question. But if she did, the door banging on her exit completely wiped out her reply.

She found Jaiden sitting in the passenger seat of the car exactly where she'd left her.

'Mandy will be here at half past,' she said.

'Perfect! I reckon a seat in the window at that Starbucks over the road should give us a good vantage point. Not to mention a great excuse for coffee.'

Saskia smiled. She liked this quirky new assistant of her Aunt Anna's. She was a bit full of herself – but it was definitely in a good way.

'I've had a text from Naz,' said Jaiden as they managed to beat a couple of mums with toddlers to the only remaining upstairs window table. She pretended not to notice when they tutted at her. 'You've probably got it too.'

Saskia checked her phone, oblivious to the ill-feeling behind her. *'Hovno!'* she muttered under her breath as she read.

Jaiden raised an eyebrow. Her knowledge of international swearwords was legendary. 'Couldn't have put it better myself!' she said, biting into the double choc chip cookie that was standing in for a very early lunch.

Mandy Simmons appeared bang on the dot of 11.30.

She was, as Sally had said, a dead-ringer for Rachel.

'Well, *that's* gotta be her!' Jaiden zoomed her phone camera up close and personal as the tall blonde tottered down the street in four inch heels. 'Her feet are gonna be killing her in those sexy little beasts by the end of the night!'

They also slowed her down nicely for the camera and Jaiden was already picking the best shot as Mandy disappeared into the bar.

'Is this Lydia Dryer?' she typed, adding a smiley, and sending it to Peter Laclan. Then she settled back into her seat. 'And now we've got a few minutes to enjoy our lattés before I have to enter the dragon's den.'

Sally chain-smoked as she paced her sitting room. Her brain felt mashed. She was still furious with Julie for siding with Rachel over Jed. But she knew that Julie had been desperate for cash. And Sally prided herself on being a good and loyal friend. Not like Rachel. The cow! And at the end of the day, good and loyal friends don't dob in their mates. She picked up her phone. Found Julie in Contacts. And hit 'dial'.

Jaiden nearly jumped out of her skin when the Pay as You Go mobile in her pocket rang. They'd got a good twenty minutes before Julie was due at the bar and she'd just been wondering whether this was a good opportunity to ask Saskia a bit more about herself.

Juggling the phone to her ear, she was just in time to hear Sally say.... *'Yeah... well... it's not like I forgive you or anything. But I just thought you need to know that Ferret's legal team have been sniffing round here asking about Mandy.... Yeah. Don't know why... No, that's all.'....* And then, after a long pause, and presumably into the smoke filled air of her empty sitting room after she had hung up. *'There... you can't say I didn't warn you... you fucking COW!'*

Saskia saw Jaiden's face change. 'Is everything alright?' she asked, anxiously.

'Nope, Sally just phoned Julie.' She was trying to think. Mandy was clearly at risk now and they'd put her there... Or more accurately ... *she* had put her there. Which meant that it was her responsibility to protect the woman. She took out her mobile and rang Laclan.'Hi Pete. Didya get the photo? Yeah? Get chance to show it to Kate yet?... Oh, okay... Well, look, there's been a development....'

A black BMW screeched into a parking space immediately outside the bar and a tall, dark haired woman in a black trouser suit and a face like thunder slammed out of it. Jaiden and Saskia winced as they looked at each other.

'.....Julie knows we're onto her.... and I think things are about to kick off here. Yeah. I know... I'm sorry. It's a long story. But can you get somebody across to Pulsations Bar... Think we might need to bring 'Lydia' in for her own protection.'

Briefly, Saskia heard a raised male voice on the other end of the phone. He seemed to be saying something about irresponsibility and lack of foresight. Jaiden cut him off.

'I'm going in there,' she said.

'No!' Saskia reached for her arm. 'Is not safe.'

'Well, if it's not safe for me. It's definitely not safe for her.'

Jaiden glugged the last of her coffee, looked longingly at the remnants of her cookie and hot-footed it down the stairs with Saskia at her heels.

They slowed down as they got to the door at Pulsations.

'Okay,' said Jaiden. 'I don't think Sally described us, so let's just go in there and suss things out nice and steady.'

Saskia nodded and gasped out what sounded like an 'Okay.' She wasn't used to living life at Jaiden's pace and she couldn't remember the last time she'd had to run anywhere. It felt – exhilarating.

'Hey... if it isn't my "Shake-Up Cocktails" Girl.' Martin bobbed up from behind the bar as they swung through the door.

He thought Saskia was looking attractively flushed and wondered if he might manage to get a date this time. Then he noticed the tall blonde dyke behind her and hoped they weren't 'together'.

'Mandy's in,' he said. 'But the boss wanted a word with her. She shouldn't be long.'

'I'll just pop to the loo,' said Jaiden. 'Get us some drinks, eh?'

She handed Saskia a tenner.

'What would you like?'

'Doesn't matter. Surprise me.'

Jaiden stopped and listened the minute she was through the door labelled 'WCs'. She knew the office must be through there too, because she had noted the slight nod of Martin's head in that direction when he'd said that Mandy was with the boss.

Faintly, up a narrow flight of uncarpeted stairs to her right, she could hear the sound of raised voices. Mandy, for the time being at least, seemed to be sticking up for herself. All things considered, Jaiden sensed that this was not a wise move.

'Well, I never wanted to go there anyway. I *told* you I wasn't any good at pretending. And she was *nice* too. She never tried it on with *me*.'

'Well maybe that's because you're such a lousy actress.' Julie's voice was lower than Mandy's. It felt measured. Frightening.

Jaiden figured the barmaid wouldn't have much experience of people like Julie. Clearly she thought she could say her piece and get away with it.

'I never pretended to be an actress!' said Mandy. 'I'm supposed to be a barmaid if you remember. But this place is going down the nick anyway. And *you*...' Jaiden could almost picture the gesture, palms up, little shake of the head. 'You have no right to talk to me like this.'

'Oh really?'

'Oh shit!'.... Jaiden began creeping very quietly up the stairs. There was a narrow landing along the top and if she managed to get there in time, she would be obscured by the door when it opened.

She texted 'Stop blonde leaving building' to Saskia as soon as she reached the top.

She was running through scenarios in her head. She figured the most likely would be a push down the stairs there and then. Though a home visit later that night might be another option... just when Mandy thought she'd said her piece and got away with it.

The building probably dated from early Victorian times. There was a small, yellow paned window at the end of the landing providing the only light on the staircase. Dust motes danced around her as she waited. Then she heard footsteps clopping towards the door. They sounded like those four inch heels of Mandy's. She pressed herself against the wall as the door handle turned. The door creaked open. And she sprang into action. 'Run!' she whispered, pulling Mandy clear as she jammed her shoulder against the door and slammed it shut again with all her might. She felt the jarring of bone against wood and clenched her teeth as Mandy clattered precariously down the stairs without a backward glance.

Julie hurled herself against the other side of the door like a Rottweiler in a cage.

'Let me out you FUCKING bitch!' She clearly thought it was Mandy who had trapped her in there. *'I'll fucking KILL you for this!'*

Jaiden was quick but she was slight and she was no match for Julie. She felt her whole body giving under the bar owner's assault on the solid Victorian door between them. Desperately, she struggled to get a grip with her feet on the age worn floorboards, bracing herself with one foot up against the banister and her back against the door. She wondered if Julie was using something very heavy to bash against the other side. She was the kind of person who would probably have a hammer or a baseball bat or something similar in there for protection. Whatever it was, it sounded like a battering ram, ringing in her ears and nearly knocking the breath out of her each time the door juddered under the full force of Julie's unleashed fury.

She felt herself weakening, and finally, she had no choice. Timing the move as best she could, she hurled herself to one side, curling into a ball away from the door.... which crashed open. And Julie, borne on her own momentum, flew through, struggling for a moment at the top of the stairs, arms flailing, bat narrowly missing Jaiden's ear as she thrashed. Then tumbling the full length of the staircase with a sound like thunder, and coming to rest, yowling and crumpled at the bottom.

'Well, Jaiden, you've really surpassed yourself *this* time.' Laclan was understandably upset.

He glared at his renegade ex-colleague, who was holding her arm gingerly. 'Does that need looking at?' he demanded.

Jaiden wouldn't have dared. 'I think it's just bruised,' she said sheepishly. 'But, hey Pete... look on the bright side. We *did* manage to find "Lydia".'

'Who's saying that your friend assaulted her, by the way... after *you* tried to shove her down the stairs.'

'I was saving her bloody life... ungrateful mare! The barman must have seen it all. He'll back us up.'

'No he won't. *He* says that his cousin Mandy came running into the bar screaming that you were attacking *their* cousin Julie and your friend grabbed her in a rugby tackle and grappled her to the floor in a completely unprovoked attack.'

It was rare for Jaiden to be stunned into silence, but she was now. She was thinking about the significance of 'Cousin Mandy' and 'Cousin Julie'.

'This isn't *the* Groves family is it?' she asked eventually. 'Willy Groves' clan?'

'At last!' Peter laughed sarcastically. 'Jaiden starts to catch up!'

'Shit!'

'Right,' said Peter. 'And you'd better hope the magistrates are sympathetic towards you. Because I'm charging you both with affray.'

Auntie Anna was also furious. 'Your father did not send you to Hunslett Ladies Academy to become a common bar-room-brawler!' she yelled.

'She was *biting* me!' Saskia protested. The bite mark was clearly visible on her forearm. The skin was broken.

It hurt like mad - as did the burgeoning black-eye, where the feral Mandy had jabbed a particularly well-aimed elbow.

'She thought you were assaulting her. If I'd been in her position I'd have bitten you too!'

Saskia looked at her Auntie Anna through her one good eye. Anna came from the Seattle side of the family and had settled in the UK after meeting her first husband at Oxford. She had been a real beauty in her youth and there was still a faint echo of all that in the fifty five year old glowering at her now, though it had been severely battered by two divorces and an over-fondness for fine food and wine.

'And it's all on the CCTV too,' said Anna. 'God knows how I'm going to get you out of *this* one.'

Jamila had just parked up at the supermarket when she saw Peter's name flashing on her mobile. She was uncomfortable with the way her heart leapt when she saw it.

'It's my day off,' she said, keeping a wary eye on the Chelsea tractor stuffed full of kids that had just pulled rather too closely into the parking space next to her.

'We've got a Jaiden situation.'

'I don't want to know.' With Sayed in one of his more distant moods at home, and the in-laws who had never liked her due that afternoon for a visit, she was ready to unleash hell on the 4 x 4 driver if she even so much as *brushed* her car as she got out.

'She's found the real Lydia Dryer.'

All thought of parking rage flew out of her head.

'Okay. I'll be with you in twenty minutes,' she said, smiling and waving at the harassed young mother as she reversed.

'So...' she said. 'Let me just check that I've got this.... Kate's client "Lydia" was actually Julie Groves' cousin Mandy.'

'Yes... Kate's identified her. That's the good news.'

'And the bad...?'

'Mandy's denying it... And Julie and Mandy are claiming that Jaiden and a friend of hers assaulted them. They've got Martin Groves as a witness and it's all on CCTV.'

'*The* Martin Groves...? The guy who put his girlfriend into Intensive Care and got off scot free because she was too frightened to press charges?'

'The very one.... Julie and Mandy's cousin Martin, in fact. He works with Mandy at Julie's Pulsations Bar.'

Jamila sighed. 'And *did* Jaiden and her friend assault them?'

'Well, they claim they were trying to stop them running away.'

'Well, *that's* a fine line, let's face it. Jaiden never could remember that she isn't actually a police officer anymore... And the Groves family will stick together like Araldite when their backs are up against the wall.'

'You're not kidding...' Peter grimaced. 'That's why they've kept one step ahead of us all these years.'

'Okay....' Jamila weighed up the options. 'Do you think there's any chance at all that Mandy or Julie could have killed Rachel?'

Laclan shook his head. 'I just can't picture it. Rachel and Julie were like sisters. I mean, Jules said she was *really* distraught about Rachel's death when she interviewed her. And we've still got no idea why Mandy was pretending to be a client of Kate's.'

Jamila weighed this up. 'Blackmail, maybe? Julie was in financial trouble. And she'll have known how important Kate's reputation is to her. "Lydia" had already started to put a complaint in. Maybe Mandy and Julie thought she'd pay to make it go away. I'd assumed that she wouldn't be all that well off as a single woman with a mortgage, but she must have *some* serious money behind her to be able to afford Anna Maxwell.'

Peter shook his head. 'No, Anna's doing this as a favour for her niece... she's a friend of Kate's partner. The one who just "assaulted" Mandy Groves, in fact, though I think you can probably guess which one of them came off worst. Actually, I doubt very much if Kate has any disposable cash but they won't have been bright enough to figure that out. And if they've just seen the public face... published author, £80 an hour private practice... the pound signs will have been lighting up in their eyes.'

'Okay, so if we can hold Mandy, at least... get fingerprints, we can check them against the fingerprint records from Kate's flat. Shame we don't still have good old fashioned, "Obtaining Services by Deception," but it *must* class as fraud. In her statement, Kate said she was seeing her as a free client, referred from the refuge.'

Peter grinned. 'Brilliant!' he said. 'And Jaiden's told me something that should help us keep Julie Groves here too...'

Julie was certainly a very cool customer. 'Classic Psychopath' thought Peter... Or maybe he should say

'Antisocial Personality Disorder' or whatever other title people were giving it these days.

Her fall down the stairs had given her a battered look... clothes ripped and smeared with dust, hair standing on end... rather like the windswept crows that used to congregate in the hawthorn trees in the field behind Peter's home when he was a child.

He wondered how Julie had got to be so cold. He'd come up against Willy Groves on several occasions and he knew how ruthless he could be. He'd seen the state of the people who tried to cross him. But with Julie, it was hard to know how much of the deadness in her was down to nature and how much to the values she'd absorbed from her family. Now, for instance, she must be badly bruised and shaken up, but you couldn't tell that by looking at her. She had the toughness of someone used to enduring pain.

'If you've got everything you need, my client would like to go home now.' The lawyer was a well known defender of the low-life of North London. His Savile Row suit and heavy gold signet ring must have been bought from the proceeds of all manner of immoral earnings. He smirked across the desk and gathered up his papers in preparation for leaving.

Julie, however, had not finished. 'So, are you going to charge those two women,' she asked. 'Or shall I put my complaint in now?'

'You don't need to do that,' said Peter, calmly. 'We've just charged them.'

'Good. I expect justice on this.'

'You'll get it, I can assure you.... Could you account for your whereabouts on the 21st October 2000?'

The lawyer rolled his eyes. 'You're scraping the bottom of the barrel now, aren't you? She must have been all of... twelve then.'

Presumably flattery was included in his fee.

'Sixteen actually,' said Peter, without looking at him. He wanted to keep eye-contact with Julie... see her reaction.

But her composure never budged as she laughed at him. 'You really haven't got a leg to stand on with this,' she said. 'So why don't you just go screw yourself?'

Sally had just settled down to see if there were any nice new men on the free dating site where she'd found Jed. New people tended to pop up there every day. She was still in her dressing gown. *Nothing wrong with a PJ day on a Saturday*, she told herself. *It wasn't like she had to go to work or anything.* The room was fogged with cigarette smoke. She had the Shopping Channel on TV for company.

She cursed when the doorbell rang.

'Sally,' said Jules Mullen. 'Do you remember me? I came and spoke to you a few days ago about the death of your friend Rachel Stiles. I'm DC Jules Mullen and this is my colleague DC Brian Crabtree.'

'Yeah...?' Sally looked at her suspiciously. 'I've told you. I don't know nothing about that.'

'Yes, Sally, and that's fine. But we'd just like to ask you some questions on a related matter.'

'Oh?' Sally felt wary of this. She didn't want to let them in.

Jules realised she was going to be kept on the doorstep this time. It didn't bother her. In fact, remembering Sally's flat, she thought that she probably preferred it.

'Okay,' she said. 'This won't take long. We'd just like to know if you can account for your whereabouts on Saturday 21st October 2000?'

The effect on Sally was instantaneous. She blinked. Then a slow insidious flush crept up her neck. 'It wasn't my fault,' she said at last, shaking her head. 'Rachel said she was gonna go get her out. How was I to know the silly cow was gonna leave her there all night?'

Jamila looked anxiously at her watch. Sayed's parents would be arriving anytime and she hadn't even got food in for them yet. Thankfully, she knew a wonderful little take-away that specialised in making things look homemade. She'd already phoned them and she could collect on the way home. She thought fleetingly that it might be easier too, to hear the food being criticised by her mother-in-law if she hadn't actually spent all afternoon preparing it herself. 'I have to go,' she said.

Peter leaned back in his seat and stretched. He smelt of Imperial Leather and coffee. And when he was tired, she felt she could still see the young boy he had once been... all gangly limbs and tousled hair and earnestness.

'I wish I could stay,' she added softly.

'Me too!' He smiled up into her eyes. 'And those fingerprints are going to take *forever* to come through.' He yawned.

'Well, it *is* Saturday teatime....'

'And we can get all the forensics we like. But they'll probably just back up our theory that Kate was stitched up with the complaint. And that, in itself gives her all the more motive for killing Rachel.'

'I know.... Look, is Jules still around.'

'Yes, I think so.'

'Why don't you get her to go back through the CCTV footage. You never know. Looking at it now, in the light of today's developments, she might just find something.'

'Good plan. I'll phone her now.'

He watched wistfully as she went, back to her life with Sayed, taking his happiness with her.

Saskia was re-evaluating her opinion of Jaiden. She was quiet at first as they snaked through the thinning early evening streets to David's house. Her aunt's voice was still ringing in her ears, though she had, at least, managed to persuade her not to phone her mum. And with the first tranche of Saturday drunks being hauled into the police station, it had taken ages to be charged and bailed. Her eye was practically closed... making driving hard, and her arm was throbbing alarmingly. Try as she might to be reassured by it, the antibiotic shot the police doctor had given her was no protection against the grim and hypochondriacal thoughts swirling through her tired mind.

'Have probably got rabies,' she said finally, making Jaiden jump.

'Nah,' Jaiden replied, following the risky strategy of trying to make light of it. 'Mandy was mad, but there was no sign of her frothing at the mouth.'

Saskia was not amused. 'Tchah...' she grumbled, glaring at Jaiden out of the corner of her good eye. 'Is *not* funny!'

'Sorry.' Jaiden raised her hands in surrender. 'But there's no point making it worse by worrying about it.'

'Is every reason... Is all your fault....' Saskia's English had all but deserted her in her rage. 'You are total loose cannons. No research... no planning... no common sense... Is all very bad in private dick!'

They remained silent for the rest of the journey. Jaiden was smarting and arguing with Saskia in her head in the way that only people who have just heard an uncomfortable home truth can do. Growing up with five brothers she'd learnt that admitting liability could be dangerous. But on this occasion she *did* think she'd made a total mess of things.

Saskia, having said her piece, was wondering if David might have a pack of frozen peas in his freezer. It might help with the black eye, at least. He looked like the kind of guy who would be meticulous about his 'five a day'. But he also looked like any vegetables he may possess would be fresh, organic and still very much in their natural packaging.

Thankfully, Naz had already thought that one through. She was used to dealing with the aftermath of brawls at the hotel. She handed Saskia a pack of peas the minute she arrived. 'I went round to 'Iceland' as soon as I heard,' she said, 'Got you some Ben and Jerry's Cookie Dough ice cream too, to say thank you. I think the pair of you were awesome... catching the fake client *and* Julie Groves all in one go.'

And she looked so grateful that Saskia's anger simply evaporated at the sight of her.

Kate, meanwhile, had reached a washed out kind of peace.

When she found Sue in the cellar, she told herself that it was all her fault. She had known immediately that her friend was collateral damage in Rachel's warped and inexplicable war against her. She believed in every inch of her that she would at some point have to pay for what she had done with Rachel while Sue was locked in that awful dark place, cold and terrified and in pain. But she had comforted herself with the idea that, at least, now she was found, Sue was safe and would be well again. She managed to hold onto that hope for several weeks. But as Sue's physical injuries healed, she sank deeper and deeper into a grim joyless place where no matter what Kate did... no matter how she tried to cheer her up... nothing worked.

And then Sue took the overdose. She'd planned it well. It was an evening when her mum was at the 'Church of the Road' helping out at the Wednesday Night Kids Club with Clare. It would have all been over by the time they returned home at eight.

Kate had never been able to explain why she suddenly felt the need to go to Sue. Maybe it had been something in her voice as she said goodbye at the bus stop on their way home from school. But Kate had been swept by a terrible feeling of dread and had abandoned her homework and told her parents she needed to borrow a book, and had run again as if her life depended on it, to find her friend.

Sue was only half conscious when she arrived. There was a note for Kate on the bedside table along with one each for her mum and Clare. She could see it all at the edge of her vision as she frantically tried to keep Sue awake, shaking her as the siren came, melding with the pulsating light on the pink flowered curtains. She'd been so frightened of what she would read in that note. She slipped it into her pocket as she followed the ambulance men and the stretcher with her friend, barely breathing, down the steep stairs.

When she opened it later, dreading what accusations would be in there, she found that Sue had written that she must not blame herself. That she had been the best friend anyone could hope to have. That Sue's sadness was for the loss of her dad and all the unfairness and cruelty of the world. She kept the note. She still had it in the fireproof box where she kept all her most important papers. But she didn't believe it. She told herself that Sue was just trying to make her feel better. And she kept right on blaming herself.

That long winter's night, when no-one knew if Sue would survive, Kate decided that the world was, indeed, a cruel and unfair place. She vowed that if Sue lived she would find a way to help her. And she decided she could never truly trust herself or anyone else, ever again.

But then Naz had come along and seen straight through her, singing to her like an idiot in the lift and taking her for ice cream when she should have been behaving like a grown-up and having sex.

And now, this strange solicitor had appeared, seemingly from nowhere. She kept assuring Kate that the fees were 'taken care of'. And she had come to see her on a Saturday evening, when surely she must have had other things she could have been doing. She told her that David had spoken to her parents, and Naz had spoken to Sue, who, apparently had now come into the police station to make a statement that might help. And bizarrely, the irritating receptionist at Horton Hill – aided and abetted by someone Kate had never even heard of - had found "Lydia" and been in a punch-up with Julie Groves.

And suddenly, Kate thought of her sixteen year-old self running through the streets of London to save her friend and she found that the guilt and self loathing that had stalked her there were almost gone and had been replaced by something approaching compassion. It shook her and softened her as she thought of it. And for the first time in days, despite the noise, despite her imprisonment, despite the strange, suspicious smelliness of the blanket she had been given, she found herself falling into a deep, exhausted sleep.

Jules stared at the fuzzy images, running them back and forth until her eyes ached. All her life she'd wanted to be a detective. By the time she was in primary school, she'd known how to lift fingerprints with sticky tape, write in invisible ink, and tell when her little brother was lying. And as she'd grown older, she'd watched and read them all, 'Prime Suspect', 'Dalziel and Pascoe,' All the 'CSI's, 'Inspector Morse.' 'Monk', the lot...

She knew that somewhere, if only she could find it, in these tapes, there must be some clue to the person who had murdered Rachel Stiles.

And she didn't, in her gut, believe that that person was Kate Ferrings.

She ran, back and forth... back and forth.

It *was* there... if only she could find it.

Her eyes were growing blurry and then, suddenly, she felt the hairs prickle on the back of her neck. She stopped the tape... rewound... ran it again.... rewound again.

Then she went to the night-time recordings, and gave a little whoop under her breath.

She picked up the phone. 'Boss,' she said, barely able to contain her excitement. 'I think I've found something.'

Laclan leaned expectantly towards the screen as Jules pointed. 'Here,' she said. 'This is Kate, getting out of the car.... And I'm pretty certain that's Mandy Simmons getting out of the passenger side... She's a bit taller than Rachel and her hair's a bit longer. Now... just watch Kate.... as she locks the car...'

Peter watched Kate as she pointed the remote. The lights flashed on the car.

'And see...' She ran forward to Kate's return... the lights flashing in greeting as she appeared out of the flat.... 'And now these are the night visits.... Watch... same car... looks like Kate... but... see!' She pointed to the screen.

Peter laughed with excitement. 'She's locking the car manually... It's the spare key... Brilliant!'

'Yeah... and I don't think this is actually Kate... It looks like her... same hair style, colouring, and the jacket is like one we found in her wardrobe... but look at her against the side of the car... this woman is a good six inches taller.'

They looked at each other appreciatively. 'Julie in a wig!' they said in unison.

Jules was honoured to be invited to Peter's desk for cappuccinos. The coffee was so strong it burned her throat. But she felt so thrilled she could barely speak anyway, so it didn't really matter.

'Okay,' he said, oblivious to how star-struck she was in his presence. 'I reckon when we get the report, we're going to find Mandy, Rachel and Julie's fingerprints all over both flats. I bet Mandy nicked Kate's spare house key, probably under cover of going to the loo at her first session. Once they'd got that, they would be able to get a copy, return the original, and pretty much have access to

Kate's place whenever they wanted it. By her own account, Kate's very much a creature of habit. She goes out for a jog every morning at 6am... back and in the shower by 6.45... She's in bed and lights out by 10.30pm every night. And she was away the whole of the weekend before the murder. It would have been so easy to come and go, 'borrow' the spare car key and jacket and take the car for a few midnight spins to Jarald Street and back. And it would have been a doddle for Rachel to go in there that last weekend and pose for those dodgy photos too. In fact, from what I hear of her, she'd probably have got quite a kick out of doing that...' Peter stopped, wondering if he'd got a bit carried away in mentioning that to a young lady, who *was* after all, his junior... He glanced cautiously at her to see if she looked shocked and hoped that the slight flush on her cheeks was due to the cappuccino steam. He decided to press on. 'It's looking almost certain that they were aiming to set Kate up on a malpractice rap so that they could blackmail her and get cash to keep the bar afloat until Rachel's divorce settlement came through.... So maybe Kate *did* snap... Maybe Mandy gave her the photos... that last day... and Kate took her back to the flat and... No, that's stupid... if *that's* what happened it would have been Mandy lying dead in that flat for five days... So...'

'So... if Kate's the killer, either Rachel must have already been in the flat. Or...

'Or both Kate and Rachel must have returned there, either together or separately, later.... And either way, Mandy... if that *is* definitely her.... must have left at some point....' Jules snatched up her cappuccino. 'I'm onto it sir.' she said, 'I'll get Brian to help.'

'I'll join you,' said Peter, abandoning the paperwork always there at the bottom of his 'to do' list, without a backward glance.

CCTV work was always laborious and that night it was unrewarding too. There was no sign of Rachel entering or leaving the flat at all that day, no sign of Mandy leaving, and no sign of Kate returning.

At midnight Peter told them all to go home.

'Let's sleep on it,' he said, wearily sliding into his thin beige summer jacket. 'Maybe things will look clearer in the morning.'

That night he dreamed of the crows in the field at home in the snow. It was Christmas and he was in the family sitting room. His mother was there, and his Uncle Bob, who used to do magic tricks. In the dream Bob looked like he did when Peter was seven and his grandma was still alive. He had a shirt with his sleeves rolled up and a mustard coloured knitted waistcoat. There was a roaring fire and cards strung over the mantelpiece on string with plastic holly at the ends. The artificial Christmas tree had all the old family baubles, including the painted glass elephant that Peter dropped and smashed when he was twelve. There was the clean pine scent of Airwick in a bottle making the tree feel real. And Bob was trying to teach Peter a card trick, but he was too clumsy to get it. He kept dropping the cards and Bob kept picking them up and trying to explain something about keys and directions.

When Peter woke with a start just after 6am, he found that he had tears in his eyes.

Jamila had also been dreaming. In her dream, she was making love to a gentle man... who held her and whispered that he loved her as he filled and merged and rose and fell with her. She woke suddenly, aroused and wrapped in the memory of her dreaming. Guiltily, and quietly, so as not to awaken the guests sleeping in the next room, she turned to Sayed and drew his drowsy morning erection into her.

Peter yawned and ruffled his hands through his hair as he filled the kettle for the first coffee of the morning. He was troubled by his dream. It had left him with a faint sense of melancholy and a feeling that somehow, somewhere, there was something he wasn't getting. He ran back over it as the kettle boiled, wondering... what was it that Bob had been trying to tell him? He put bread in the toaster and spooned ground coffee into the cafetiere, breathing in the scent as he always did. He wondered whether he should have Marmite or marmalade on his toast, and whether he should take it all back to bed or sit at the kitchen table.

He ran back over the dream, trawling through his memory to the actual day.... All those years ago now... Remembering the warmth of the fire on his cheeks, and Bob saying....

'Misdirection is the key.' And then, when he'd realised that Peter hadn't understood the big word. *'You've got to get them to look where you want them to look, while you're doing what you don't want them to see.'*

Of course!... He shook his head at his own stupidity.

All thought of returning to bed fled from his thoughts. Pouring a mug of coffee and hurriedly smearing Benecol on his toast, Peter headed upstairs, stripped out of his dressing gown as he ate, and made for the shower.

Cavendish Rd was just emerging from its Sunday morning lie-in when Peter arrived. He spotted a smart looking young man loading a sports bag into his car and waited for him to leave so that he could have the parking space for his Ford Mondeo. The intermingled smells of bacon and egg and simmering curry goat wafted through the open car window as he waited. The faint sound of smooth jazz was drifting from one of the flats further up the road. It was a sound that Peter always associated with the night-time. It felt incongruous on the warm morning air, but he quite liked it none the less. As he got out of the car and paced out the numbers of the houses, he could see that Mrs Morgan was already up and in her kitchen at the back of Number 5, Jarald Street. He could also, now, see clearly, over the gate and through the washing carousel and lilac bushes of the back garden, the metal railings of what must surely be stone steps leading down to the basement back door. The whole area had been photographed when they all still thought this was likely to be a suicide. But then he and Jamila and their team had been distracted to the front of the house by their search for evidence for or against Kate Ferrings. He was furious with himself. And the excuse of 'pressure of work', which actually was genuine enough, just didn't wash with him at all.

Behind him, he heard a gate click, followed by the distinctive 'chunk... chunk... chunk...' of a ball being kicked against a garage door.

He turned to look at the lad, maybe eleven or twelve, with stubbly blonde hair and a grey threadbare tracksuit.

'Morning,' he said.

'Hey!' The lad caught the ball expertly as it bounced back to him. He tucked it under his arm. 'You one o'them murder tourists?' he asked in a surprisingly gruff voice as he ambled over to Peter's side and nodded across at Number 5.

'No... I'm from the police. Do you often play here?'

The lad bristled. 'There's no law against it. It's my mum's garage.'

Peter nodded. 'Was just wondering if you saw much of *her* while you were out here?'

'Who... the bird what was murdered?'

'Yeah.'

The lad shoved out his chest. 'Saw her coming and going. She was hot. A bit old. But I like 'em that way. More grateful.'

'Yeah, yeah,' said Peter. 'Save it for your mates.'

He was unabashed. 'Reckon I must have been practically the last person to see her alive. Didn't know it then though.'

'You saw her then... that Monday?'

'Yeah... First week of school holidays. That dark-haired mate of hers dropped her back about four. I remember 'cos she looked half-cut. She was staggering a bit and the friend parked up here in front of the garages and went in with her. She was in there for about an hour. My mum was bloody ranting. She needed to get out for work and she was blocked in by that bloody great Beamer. She was well narked.' The lad looked at him with his head cocked to one side. 'Gruesome was it?'

'Yes,' said Peter. 'It's always gruesome... Did you see anybody else leaving the house that day? Apart from the dark haired friend, that is.'

The lad pulled on his lip. 'It's a long time ago,' he said.

'Yeah,' Peter nodded and waited. He could see that he was thinking.

'*She* went out in the morning,' he said eventually. 'Her mate with the Beamer picked her up. I remember, cos she just sat in the middle of the street, tooting on her horn.'

'Can you remember what time that was?'

'Bout ten-ish. The bin men couldn't get past her, so she had to pull in here again to let 'em through. But she didn't get out that time.'

'Did anybody else go in or come out?'

'Only the other blonde. She came out about twelve o'clock. Went up towards the High Street.'

'Had you seen her around here before?'

'Nah, just that once. She wasn't as pretty as the other one.'

Peter felt himself becoming very still. He'd always found that the truth was easily scared away if you pounced on it too soon.

'Have you given us a statement about what you saw?' He asked this casually, as if it didn't matter really.

'Nah... we were on holiday when they found her... and you've got somebody for it anyway, an't ya... That psycho therapist... Geddit... *psycho* therapist?!' He laughed at his own joke.

Laclan smiled, just to keep him on side. 'Mm... Well, actually, there have been some developments since then... Look... is your mum in now?'

Peter probably shouldn't have, but he bought Jaiden a coffee anyway.

'So the blackmail and the murder weren't actually connected?' she said.

'Only in so far as they featured some of the same players.'

'And the stage was already perfectly set for Kate to take the rap.'

'Yes, once Julie had a spare key for Kate's place I'm guessing she and Rachel will have come and gone pretty much as they pleased. The indecent photos of Rachel were taken on Julie's phone. She hadn't even tried to delete them. They took them while Kate was at a conference in Leeds and I imagine they were planning on using them to extort money out of her once they'd got the complaint underway.... It was clever, and who knows... it might even have worked. They could certainly have wrecked her career with all *that* lot. Then Julie killed Rachel. I think she probably planned it. She's cold like that. My guess is that she'd already drugged her before she got home and just added diazepam to the tea that Kate had made earlier for Mandy. She probably planted Rachel's phone and the envelope of photos the next morning while Kate was out jogging... We're getting the closest CCTV for Kate's street now, but I'm sure Julie's car will be on there. It must have been the longest week of her life waiting for someone to find the body. But then she swung into action - tipped us off about Kate taking Mandy back to the flat.... probably tipped off the newspapers too. She had us fooled for a while. But thankfully we got there in the end.'

Jaiden whistled. 'But why?' she asked. 'They were life-long buddies. I don't get it.'

'I was struggling with that one myself. Then I remembered what Mike, Rachel's husband said when we interviewed him. He said that Rachel was coming home.

She was fed up with Jed and fed up with Mrs Morgan and she wanted to go back to him.'

'Stuffing the prospect of the divorce settlement Julie was banking on to prop up Pulsations, right?'

'Exactly... Let's face it. They weren't going to get much of a re-launch out of any money they managed to get out of Kate. And I'm guessing it wasn't only about the money. Julie will have felt betrayed by Rachel, I'm sure... She'd sided with her against Sally. And now Rachel was running out on her too. If there's one thing the Groves' are into, it's loyalty. You just don't cross 'em and get away with it.'

Jaiden leaned back in her swivel chair and crossed her arms. 'Seems like our work here is done,' she said. 'Have you released Kate yet?'

'Jamila's just sorting the admin. As you know that's not my strong suit.'

'Me neither mate. Don't know how you stick it personally.... And speaking of the lovely Jamila, I can't help but notice that you're still carrying a torch for her.' She felt concerned for him, though she broached the subject lightly.

He busied himself with his computer and avoided her eye.

She took this as confirmation.

'And she hasn't noticed yet that Sayed's been having an affair for the last two years?'

'Love is blind,' he said.

'You don't ever think of just telling her?'

He looked at her as if she'd gone mad. 'And break her heart?' he asked. 'How the hell can I do *that* when I love her so much?'

Naz could feel her stomach churning as she leaned against the railings outside the police station waiting for her lover to be released.

It was a warm day – sunny – reminding her of that afternoon, a lifetime ago, it seemed, when she'd first met Kate. She'd looked so lovely standing there, all hot and grumpy at the thought of having her conference at Horton Hill. And Naz could never have imagined where that meeting was destined to take her.

Now the sounds of a different summer's day drifted around her. A drunk sat on the edge of the pavement nursing a bottle in a paper bag. He was singing a ramshackle, slurred version of 'Fog on the Tyne', though he didn't sound like a Geordie and he only seemed to know the chorus. After six times through, it was getting to be irritating. Naz closed her eyes for a moment, feeling almost drowsy now that the worst of all this was over. On the busy main road, just round the corner, the car tyres on the hot tarmac sounded like waves on a shingle beach. Maybe if Kate still wanted her, they could go away on holiday together... lie in the sun... walk along the water's edge... kiss in the moonlight.... *If* Kate still wanted her.

There was an estate of high rise flats opposite. She thought, as she always did, about all those other lives, those other points of view. There were the neat windows where people had nice curtains and flowers. The windows with a message – a Tottenham scarf, a Scottish flag, a sign saying 'Keep Knives Off our Streets'... And the ones that just stared out blankly into the world. No curtains, no flowers, no message... nothing. She wondered whether anyone lived in those at all.

Somewhere within the estate, she could hear the gruff voices of lads playing football. They reminded her of walking in the park with Kate, not so very far from here. That was the day her feelings had run away from her and tumbled headlong into love.

She figured that Kate would be appearing any minute now. A hush had fallen over the welcoming party, expectant... waiting.

Saskia was her usual, morose self, leaning back against the railings, a half smoked cigarette smouldering in her hand. She glowered at the drunk, who looked just about to start up his song again, and he must have felt her eyes boring into him, because he suddenly hauled himself to his feet and staggered away down the road, waving his bottle in a final dramatic flourish as he zigzagged slowly out of sight.

David was sitting on the bonnet of his car, ankles crossed, in pale denim jeans and sneakers. He was, maybe, in his late fifties, but there, in that pose, he looked like a teenager in a sixties movie. A younger guy in shorts and shades glanced back over his shoulder at him as he passed. Naz imagined he must have men throwing themselves at him all the time. But she'd seen all of the ways he still loved the beautiful man who smiled out from photographs everywhere around his house. And she knew he would choose to spend the rest of his life alone.

Susan was quiet now too. She had greeted her like an old friend, though it was only yesterday that they'd met. Naz could tell that she was an ally. She wanted Kate to be happy. She'd come with her partner Brenda, a tall, sinewy teacher in austere, heavy framed glasses, who she introduced affectionately as 'The Missus.' Her mood seemed lighter than when Naz had last seen her and she'd winked at her as she got out of their car. It was as if a terrible weight had been lifted from her shoulders. 'We'll soon have her back now,' she'd said to everyone. It seemed like she'd been waiting for that for a very long time.

Jamila had been keen to accompany Kate out of the building. It felt important and symbolic to return her to her friends.

'I am truly sorry,' she said, as they reached the door.

'No... you shouldn't be... I'm sorry I lashed out at you. I didn't mean to.'

The sun dazzled her eyes as she stepped back out into the world.

Kate heard what sounded like a cheer. Then she heard running feet and felt Sue's arms around her and Brenda patting her on the back. She caught sight of David, hopping off the bonnet of his car and standing, just a little bit removed, waiting to see if she would want to come to him. She couldn't see Naz and she tried to tell herself that she didn't mind.

'They destroyed *themselves* in the end,' said Sue, exhilarated by her own part in it and crying and laughing all at once.

Kate held onto her and thanked her. 'I should phone my parents,' she said. 'They must have been worried sick.'

'They're fine,' smiled Sue. 'I've already done it. They're coming across to David's for tea. And I reckon you might as well bite the bullet and tell 'em about the girlfriend while they're still in shock.' She nodded, very gently towards the railings where Naz stood, too scared to move, watching and waiting.

Kate felt a rush of relief that took her breath away. She still had an arm around Sue, who was saying something about her being a 'dark horse'... but her attention had leapt across to Naz, who looked so small and vulnerable and hesitant standing there.... And suddenly she couldn't hear anything except the sound of her heart, telling her how very much she loved the sweet-natured young woman who had found her on a hot, rubbish-strewn street in late July and reached out unquestioningly to save her. 'Oh God,' she thought. 'What will I do if she doesn't want me now?'

Tears sprang into her eyes at the thought.

And almost without knowing how, Naz crossed the space between them and wrapped Kate safe into her arms at last.

Like all good legal teams, Jaiden and Anna had flanked Kate as they came out of the police station. Now they were supposed to shake a few hands, fade quietly into the background, and leave. But Anna had a taste for good-looking men and she did a double-take when she spotted David. 'Is *that* David Cohen?' she asked, shaking her hair back in an unconsciously coquettish gesture. 'I think I'll just go and introduce myself.'

Jaiden smiled at Saskia, 'Poor David,' she said. 'Do you think he's up to handling your Auntie Anna in full seduction mode?'

Saskia dragged her eyes away from Naz and Kate, and looked across at her aunt. Over the years she'd lost track of all the unattainable men Anna had fancied.... gay, married, celibate, one particularly unpleasant psychopath... and a whole raft of plain, simple commitment-phobes. She'd even managed to get a couple of them down the aisle, though they hadn't stuck around for very long after that. With her own rather depressing romantic track record, Saskia had always wondered if she'd inherited the same gene, but now it crossed her mind that maybe she'd just been looking for love in the wrong place all along.

'He'll be fine,' she said, distractedly. She was watching Naz holding Kate, breathing her in, kissing her, saying all those sweet, soft, private things that lovers say when they've been parted for too long.

Jaiden saw the pain in her eyes as she watched. 'Why do they always go for the wrong woman?' she asked softly, trying to be sympathetic.

'What do you mean?'

'Just.... that we love 'em but they always seem to fall for someone else.'

Saskia looked mortified. 'I am *not* in love with Naz,' she said. 'If that is what you mean.' She hated the idea of being so transparent. She didn't want to be pitied by anyone.

'Oh... sorry... no... of course not...' Jaiden knew that she hadn't been mistaken, but she also knew better than to push it. She leaned back against the railings and busied herself with a roll-up. 'So... moving on from that particularly embarrassing faux pas... What happens next?'

'Don't know. Will depend what Kate would like. Tea with parents, I think. Then hot shower and bed might be first choice.' Saskia's English had fled to the hills again in confusion.

'I meant *you*. What will *you* do now that all this is sorted?'

Saskia hesitated. This was something she'd been putting off thinking about.

'I will go home to my mother in Bratislava,' she said, eventually.

'And then?'

'Then I will work in the family business and marry some man who wants me for my money. Maybe, if the prenuptial agreement is strong, he will stay with me and treat me well.'

Kate was holding Naz's hand as she spoke to David. It was as if she never wanted to let her go.

'Or you could stay here and work with Anna and me.'

Saskia stared at her. She hadn't been expecting that.

'I think you'd enjoy it. You're brilliant undercover. We could have a lot of fun. And I'm sure Anna would love to have you around.'

'Is crazy idea,' said Saskia. 'And you are crazy woman.'

'Well, it's good to be a little crazy sometimes. Why not mull it over, at least?' Jaiden cast a cheeky look out of the corner of her eye. She licked her Rizla paper, pulled the loose strands of tobacco from the ends...

Saskia eyed her suspiciously. Jaiden thought she looked very cute when she took on that fierce, paranoid look. Like she was trying to be tough, and wasn't.

And, despite herself, Saskia thought that Jaiden was rather cute too. Nothing like Naz of course, but tall and sparky and a bit wild, like you'd never get bored with her but she'd always be there for you if you needed her to be. As she looked at her like that, she thought it might be rather nice to consider Jaiden's offer.

Over by David's car the small group was starting to look ready to move.

'We're all going back to my place now,' he called. 'I hope you'll both join us?'

'Yes – will come,' Saskia replied. Then dropping her voice, she turned to Jaiden who was still waiting for an answer to her proposal. 'And afterwards I might.... just might... consider going undercover with you.'

Printed in Poland
by Amazon Fulfillment
Poland Sp. z o.o., Wrocław